An Inhabitant
of the Planet Mars

An Inhabitant
of the Planet Mars

by
Henri de Parville

Translated by
Brian Stableford,
with an Introduction and Afterword

A Black Coat Press Book

ISBN 978-1-934543-45-0. First Printing June 2008. Published
by Black Coat Press, an imprint of Hollywood Comics.com,
LLC, P.O. Box 17270, Encino, CA 91416. All rights reserved.
Except for review purposes, no part of this book may be reproduced or transmitted in any form or by any means, elec-
tronic or mechanical, including photocopying, recording, or by
any information storage and retrieval system, without permission in writing from the publisher. The stories and characters
depicted in this novel are entirely fictional. Printed in the
United States of America.

Introduction

Henri de Parville's *Un habitant de la planète Mars*, here translated as *An Inhabitant of the Planet Mars*, was originally published by "J. Hetzel" (Pierre-Jules Hetzel) in May 1865. The genesis of the work was an article in the form of a letter that had appeared in the daily newspaper *Le Pays* on June 17, 1864. The letter was signed "A. Lomon," that being the name of the paper's American correspondent, responsible for reporting on the progress of the Civil War. (In those days, newspaper correspondents really did communicate by letter, which is why the article was presented in that form.) The article revealed that an "aerolith"—a meteorite, in modern terminology—excavated from an ancient geological stratum in Colorado by an oil prospector had turned out to contain a mummified humanoid, believed to originate from the planet Mars. The article—which was, of course, a hoax—caused something of a stir among the paper's readers, and demanded a follow-up, which duly appeared a few days later. By that time, it was on open secret that the actual author of the original article had been the paper's science correspondent, Henri de Parville.

The immediate inspiration of Parville's hoax was a combination of circumstances deriving from the fall of a stony meteorite—a "carboanceous chondrite" quite unlike the more familiar metallic "siderites"—some 20 fragments of which were recovered near the French town of Orgueil on May 14, 1864. The various fragments were distributed to many scientific institutions, including one in Chicago in the USA, where they were examined by numerous scientists. In France, however, they took on a particular significance in the context of a controversy that had been bubbling away for five years, in which one of the contenders, Louis Pasteur, had delivered what he believed to be a lethal blow a few weeks earlier, on April 7. On that day, Pasteur had delivered an address to a regular "scientific soirée" at the Sorbonne in which he reported the results of a series of experiments that he had carried out in order to disprove the theory of spontaneous generation championed by his rival, Félix-Archimède Pouchet. Parville, as an ambitious scientific journalist, would certainly have been present at the soirée, on the bench set aside for the press, and would have seen Pouchet walk out, complaining that the audience was prejudiced against him.

Pouchet, who preferred to call his thesis "*hétérogénie*" [heterogenesis] had earlier conducted a series of experiments in which he concocted mixtures of the various materials he thought necessary to the spontaneous generation of life and left them alone for a while; in every case, living creatures eventually appeared. Organic chemistry was then in its infancy, and microbiology was still working under the severe handicap of microscopes whose acuity was limited by chromatic aberration; bacteria were not yet included on the official roster of living organisms, although the suspicion that organisms too tiny to be visible—as yet—was widespread. Pasteur was convinced that Pouchet's experiments had been contaminated by such invisible "germs" and repeated them, sterilizing all the mixtures with heat, then sealing half the containing vessels to avoid the possibility of external contamination. The unsealed vessels "generated" life while the sealed ones did not—this was what Pasteur

6

reported to the soirée, along with the claim that he had proved that spontaneous generation did not occur.

Pasteur's address became famous—the full text can be read on the internet, in French and English—and was widely cited as a classic application of the experimental method, although the impossibility of proving a negative meant that he had really only provided evidence that Pouchet's experiments could have been subject to external contamination. Pouchet continued to fight his corner until he died, and was not entirely without sympathy in the French scientific community. Although Pouchet has been largely forgotten in the interim, he had a considerable reputation at the time as a popularizer of science, and one element of his retaliation to Pasteur's address was the publication in 1865 of *L'univers*, a lavishly-illustrated summarization of contemporary ideas regarding the cosmos, its origin and development, which was reprinted several times. Perhaps more significantly, he was also one of the leading French supporters of Charles Darwin, who had published *The Origin of Species* in 1859, the year that the Pouchet-Pasteur feud had kicked off.

Although Pasteur's victory was, and still is, regarded as a heroic triumph science over superstition—or at least over pseudoscience—his convictions owed as much to his Catholic faith and his antipathy to Darwinism as to his scientific principles. He was opposed to both heterogenesis and natural selection on the grounds that they were essentially "materialistic," threatening the elimination of God's creative role in the history of the universe. His diehard belief in invisible "germs"—which also led to his revolutionizing the theory of disease and thus laying the foundations of modern medicine—was, in essence, a means of saving God's creativity from the

7

menace of a materialistic model of life's emergence. He would presumably have been disappointed had he been able to anticipate that his own theories would one day be considered to be pillars of materialism, sidelining God just as rudely as he considered Pouchet to have done.

The relevance of all this to the Orgueil meteorite—and thus to Parville's hoax—was that the scientists examining the fragments of the chondrite soon began to report the existence within it of organic materials. The finding was initially reported on May 31 by a scientist who signed his papers S. Cloëz, but it was rapidly confirmed by others, including Marcellin Berthelot and Louis Pasteur. This discovery seemed to many observers and commentators to have a significant bearing on the still-hot topic of spontaneous generation, especially if—as Cloëz and others suggested—the organic materials were fossils: the remains of long-dead living creatures. The scientific significance of fossils had been considerably boosted in the early 19th century by fierce arguments about the true age of the Earth and the evolution of life on its surface, whose fervor had recently been refueled by *The Origin of Species*; their newsworthiness had been further enhanced by a craze for "dinosaur-hunting" that was raging in the USA alongside, and despite, the Civil War.

The extraterrestrial origin of meteorites had been a hot topic of controversy itself at the beginning of the 19th century, and although it was largely settled by 1864, there was no universally-agreed theory as to exactly where they originated, or why they differed in composition. If some contained fossils, where could those fossils possibly have come from? If the original organisms had sprung from Pasteurian "germs," where had the germs originated? It seemed to some interested parties that, if there really was, or ever had been, life inside "*bolides*"—the hypothetical spacefaring bodies that were supposed to give rise to meteorites—then spontaneous generation offered a more plausible explanation than a separate and deliberate act of divine creation, or what later came to be known as the "panspermia hypothesis": the notion that life originated elsewhere in the universe had reached Earth—and many other planets—by means of a migration.

At any rate, the potential significance of the Orgueil meteorite's organic contents briefly became a significant source of speculation in the burgeoning world of French scientific journalism. The publicity given to the analyses of the fragments and the presence within them of organic material not only prompted Parville's hoax but provided it with a media environment that guaranteed it a measure of superficial plausibility. When the decision was made to expand the two newspaper articles into a book, it was entirely natural that Parville should elect to construct an imaginary "scientific commission" not unlike the one that had sat in judgment over Pasteur's experiments at the Sorbonne, which would not only settle the question as to whether the aerolith containing a mummified human really had come from Mars, but examine what that conclusion might imply for contemporary science's model of the universe and the evolutionary process, with particular reference to the role therein of spontaneous generation. It is possible that Parville had not made up his own mind about the issue when he started out on he extrapolation, and that he used the imaginary debate to clarify his own thoughts and to decide where he stood—for the time being, at least.

Parville evidently began to struggle with the task of extrapolating his original article as soon as he was required by popular demand to write as follow-up piece. He had, in effect, already set out the basic idea in its entirety; the second letter could only reiterate it and add some relatively trivial additional details. Although the notion of describing the proceedings of a scientific conference summoned to study and discuss the discovery must have seemed both obvious and attractive to him, he found considerable practical difficulty in formulating that project.

The first chapter of the extrapolation clearly intends to develop the description of the conference as a satire on the conduct of contemporary scientists; it mostly consists of a series of more-or-less brief descriptions of eccentric stereotypes. It is possible that Parville cannibalized other writings in its composition; the anecdotal description of Mr. Stek might well have been co-opted from elsewhere. He soon decided—or was advised by his publisher—that he was on the wrong track, and, rather than begin again, abruptly changed direction. His subsequent attempts at satirical humor were tokenistic, and he settled down to the more earnest business of constructing a summary account of—quite literally—life, the universe and everything.

Parville never wrote anything else as expansive as the cosmic vision featured in *Un habitant de la planète Mars*. The fact that he was writing fiction, putting his ideas into the mouths of hypothetical individuals, gave him a freedom to speculate and associate disparate ideas that he did not allow himself in his customary reportage. The struggle he experienced in fictionalizing the material, however, illustrated one of the key difficulties under which the hybrid genre of "science fiction" has always labored: the fact that any authorial concession to the primary narrative convention of mimetic representation (usually summarized as "show, don't tell") tends to have a focusing effect that is not easily suited to the discussion of scientific issues, especially those involving the development of Grand Theory. In general, story-telling techniques make a much better metaphorical microscope than telescope, while non-fictional formats are far more amenable to the opposite tendency. By keeping his concessions to narrative design to an absolute minimum, though, Parville achieved a particular combination of quasi-non-fictional technique and speculative ambition that was exceedingly rare at the time, although it is echoed in numerous 20th century works of "visionary non-fiction," perhaps most artfully in the works of Loren Eiseley.

Inevitably, everything that Parville thought about the nature of the universe was eventually falsified by the progress of scientific knowledge. His notion of how the cosmos is organized and the character of the interconnecting threads that bind it into a coherent whole were based on false assumptions, of whose falseness he could not yet have been aware. The whole ideative edifice is, in retrospect, nothing but a work of fantastic fiction. That does not mean, however, that it was in any way unintelligent; nor does it mean that it became uninteresting the moment the falsity of its core assumptions was revealed by the further theoretical progress of geology, physics and organic chemistry. Indeed, it is arguable that Parville's cosmic vision is as useful an artifact in the archaeology of knowledge as his hypothetical meteorite would have been to its discoverers.

In particular, the essay that Parville extrapolated from his initial hoax allows modern readers to perceive how strangely misleading incomplete knowledge can be, how easy it is to build a mistaken edifice of speculation, quite conscientiously, on actual discoveries, and—perhaps most interestingly of all—how cultural factors work on the interpretation of scientific data to produce particular perspectives. Parville's cosmic vision is a distinctively French vision, quite different in significant ways from the kindred visions built in Britain by Robert Hunt, in *The Poetry of Science* (1848), and in America by Edgar Allan Poe, in *Eureka* (1848). The fact that those distinctive features also show up in the work of his rival popularizer, Camille Flammarion, and were preserved in a considerable fraction of subsequent French scientific romance—though not the works of Jules Verne and his meeker imitators—is due at least as much to a common intellectual background as to any direct influence.

The author of *Un habitant de la planète Mars* was born François-Henri Peudefer in Evreux in 1838. After completing his education at the Ecole des Mines—which specialized in the education of would-be mining engineers, although it had perforce to take some interest in more theoretical issues in geological science—he joined a scientific expedition to the Americas, spending time in Central America and the Southern USA before returning to France in 1860. He immediately embarked on a career as a science journalist, eventually writing articles for many of the leading periodicals of the day. His position with *Le Pays* was the first of any significance, and he was still building his career when he produced his hoax article in 1864, but he subsequently went from strength to strength, working for *Le Constitutionnel, La Patrie* and *Le Moniteur*, before becoming the editor of *Science pour tous* and the science correspondent of the *Journal des Débats*. He joined the editorial staff of *La Nature* soon after its foundation in 1873, and played a significant role in its direction during the final decades of the century.

Like many other men of his century who claimed descent from extinct noble families, Peudefer was ambitious to reclaim an appearance of aristocratic status, and began signing himself "Henri de Parville" from the outset of his career, although he was not granted the right by official decree until December 1865 (according to Larousse; a rival encyclopedia has 1869). In addition to his work for periodicals he produced an annual series of *Causeries scientifiques* [Scientific Chats] launched in 1861, which offered an informal and sometimes witty explanatory survey of each year's scientific progress, and eventually acquired a large readership. In the same year that *Un habitant de la planète Mars* appeared he published a substantial account of *Découvertes et industries moderne* [Modern Discoveries and Industries] and he went on to produce other significant popularizations, notably one of the guidebooks to *L'Exposition Universelle de 1867*; subsequently, he provided the same service for the Exposition of 1889.

Parville was invited as an honored guest to the first screening by the Lumière brothers of their epoch-making film of a train entering a railway station on December 28, 1895, and the comments that he subsequently gave to the press were so widely reproduced that they eventually eclipsed everything else he wrote—they are still quoted in many websites. He retired from active journalism in the early years of the 20th century, eventually dying in 1909. He was sufficiently famous and well-respected to be posthumously honored by the foundation of a Prix

Henri de Parville by the Académie des Sciences, which is still awarded annually.

This translation has been made from the version of the text produced by *Ebooks libres et gratuits* and distributed via their website, *ebooksgratuits.com*. I have not been able to compare it with the original, but I strongly suspect that most, if not all, of the typographical errors and misspellings contained in the neatly reset text were carried forward from the Hetzel edition. I have corrected numerous trivial errors of this sort and have unified the forms of several names that are given in different versions at different points of the text.

Translation of antique speculative texts is always problematic because of their use of obsolete terminology, but I have attempted rigorously to avoid the temptation to substitute terms of more recent provenance, however apt they might seem. This results in the preservation in my version of such awkward phrases as "quantity of motion" (from *quantité de mouvement*), for which most modern texts—of a visionary as well as a scientific nature—would certainly substitute "energy," but it would have distorted the character of the text to do otherwise. I have, for the same reason, dutifully preserved the usage of "inhabitant of the planet Mars" rather than substitute "Martian," although it might be the inherent tendency of the French language—which always uses formulations of the sort *X de Y* where English routinely uses contracted formulations—that led Parville to use that laborious formula, rather than any enigmatically conscientious determination on his part to refrain from coining the now-familiar French word *Martien*.

Further problems arose from the fact that Parville's text is so abundantly footnoted, and that some of his footnotes require footnoting themselves if they are to be of much use to modern readers; I have prefaced all my translations of his footnotes with an introductory identifier and have placed direct translations thereof in inverted commas, so as to distinguish them from my supplementary comments and my own notes. I hope that the footnotes to this edition, although they are very extensive indeed, will allow the text to be read with an appropriate understanding of context. Some further comments on the work's situation within the development of French scientific romance and contemporary scientific knowledge are supplied in the afterword.

Brian Stableford

An Inhabitant of the Planet Mars

Preface

The letters that compose this book were addressed to us successively in a fashion that was, to say the very least, singular.

At dawn, after waking up, almost every day for a fortnight, on a regular basis, we found a new letter with an American postmark on our work-desk, already open.

The origin of this mysterious correspondence remains unknown to us, despite the most scrupulous research.

The first two were inserted in an evening newspaper. Their appearance caused an emotion of excitement in all our minds at the time, which has not yet calmed in England and Germany. Details of the information they contained were reproduced by almost all the newspapers in Europe, which confirmed or added to them.

We decided today to publish the others. As they complete the preceding items and treat philosophical and scientific matters that are currently highly controversial, such as the origin of species, the transformation of creatures, spontaneous generation and the plurality of worlds, we think that they will be read with some interest by all thinking men and advanced minds.

We reproduce them here absolutely as we received them, neither omitting anything nor adding anything. We have only permitted ourselves to annotate those passages which demanded clarification or required correction.

H. de P.

LETTER I

Correspondence from Richmond. An unprecedented discovery. Widespread rumors in America. In which a search is made for oil and a mummy is discovered. A buried aerolith. Excitement in the scientific world. A petrified man. Where has he come from? A fossiliferous tomb. Four planets and a conclusion. An inhabitant of another world.

A scientific discovery of capital importance has been made in the Arapaho region a few miles from James Peak.[1] A rich landowner in the neighborhood, Mr. Paxton, had begun digging for oil. One morning, the pick-axe rebounded from an extremely hard rock; the alluvial deposit having been traversed, a carboniferous layer had been reached and the work was continuing in the paleozooic stratum.[2] It was thought that a metal seam had been reached and a drill was brought into play; it sent back a sort of conglomerate formed of traprock, porphyry, quartz crystals and metallic composites.

Mr. Davis, a highly distinguished geologist from Pittsburgh, begged Mr. Paxton to follow this accumulation, and, after a fortnight's work, the upper part of an enormous slightly ovoid mass had been stripped bare. Its composition is distinct not only from that of the neigh-

---

[1] James Peak is in Gilpin County, Colorado. Parville has "Arrapahys" rather than Arapaho, the former being a French version used in some early 19th century reference books.

[2] Parville: "So-called because it is the first in which traces of organisms are discovered."

boring rocks but from any specimen discovered on our globe until now.

The mass measures about 85 yards in its largest diameter and 30 in its smallest. Enormous saccharoid fractures are visible within it, making anfranctuosities and doubtless indicating the places where fragments of it must have been explosively detached. The entire mass is coated on the outside with a sort of black enamel of variable thickness comprised of metallic silicates. Beneath this coat, according to Mr. Davis, the rock is formed of alkaline and earthen silicates of iron, manganese, nickel, cobalt, tungsten, copper, tin, arsenic, sulfur, alkaline chlorides, ammonium chlorohydrate, traces of silver chloride, traces of cesium and large quantities of graphite, with a gaseous layer interposed at a depth of one meter, comprising nitrogen, carbon dioxide, hydrogen sulfide and hydrogen arsenide.

The extremely peculiar composition of this mass left the geologists in no doubt. The mass encountered at the foot of James Peak is not of terrestrial origin; it is an aerolith, and certainly the most curious ever seen, firstly by virtue of its composition and its large volume, but more especially because of its situation. Never before has it been possible to discover any kind of aerolith in the succession of ancient strata.

It is rare for strokes of good luck to occur singly. A second discovery was bound to follow the first, and its importance is such that, at the time of writing, it is causing an even greater stir among the country's intelligentsia. The war has almost been forgotten, and curiosity-seekers are flocking to the Arapaho region.

A commission has been established in the neighborhood to examine the Paxton/David aerolith; it had the good idea of piercing the mass along the axis of its larger diameter. At a depth of four meters the composition changed noticeably. Up to that point, the rock presented traces of fusion; in its course through our atmosphere, the bolide had heated up and its surface had melted. Beyond that depth, however, the material became porphyroid, with very large crystals, about the size of an egg, composed of amphibole,[3] quartz or feldspar. This was followed by quartzite, with veins of iron and copper. At seven meters, the composition changed to granite with silver crystals. At 20 meters, the drill was advancing slowly through ophite [4] when the bit suddenly screeched and rebounded. It simultaneously lost purchase and jumped, making a hollow sound, ending up a few meters further down. A jet of unbreathable gas emerged, reaching the workmen.

The hole made by the drill was enlarged and a shaft was hollowed out. It took no less than ten days—ten days of waiting and unsatisfied curiosity!

Finally, Mr. John Paxton, the son of the landowner, and Mr. Davis went down to the bottom of the hole. There were a few minutes of hesitation before they came back. They were both very pale. Mr. Paxton was carrying a sort of stout amphora made of white metal—silver and zinc—pockmarked with little holes and bizarre designs.

Whence came this vase? What was it doing at the bottom of the shaft? Those were the questions pressing on everyone's lips.

---

[3] Parville: "A mineral of variable color, formed of silica, magnesium, calcium carbonate and ferrous oxide."
[4] Parville: "A variety of rock formed of feldspar and silica, calcium carbonate, magnesium, iron oxides and manganese."

"At the bottom of the hole," the two explorers reported, "we found the amphora embedded horizontally in the ophite; the drill-bit had touched it and partially detached it; about six feet lowers down, our feet came to rest on a metal sheet, which resonated dully and seemed to be encased in the rock. Above it and to the left, but too deeply embedded in the rock for us to be able to extract them, we made out several more metal amphorae, with yellow rods of some sort."

Too much curiosity had been excited for the matter to rest there. The hole at the bottom of the shaft was enlarged until the metal covering was fully exposed. It was dented all over, granulated, oxidized, black in places and even melted. They worked all night, but it was not until the evening of the third day that the metal plate became detachable. They proceeded carefully, for fear of inflammable gas, but there was no explosion when the lamps were sent down. Two workmen and Messrs. John Paxton, Davis and Murchison removed the heavy plate, which was about six feet wide.

The lamps shone a yellowish light into the excavation and illuminated it. The watching men could not retrain a cry of astonishment. Before their eyes was a rectangular space about three feet deep and six feet wide, most certainly hewn out of granite. The empty space was heaped almost everywhere with calcareous concretions, something like stalagmites, which sparkled in the lamplight. In the center, a human form of short stature, seemingly enveloped in a calcareous shroud, was clearly visible. He was lying down, fully extended, and measured scarcely four feet in height. His slightly-raised head vanished into a cushion of calcium carbonate and his legs also disappeared beneath the calcareous envelope.

It was very difficult to extract this stony tomb from its granite walls, and it was necessary to enlarge the shaft to bring it up to the surface. The calcium carbonate had molded itself to the gap and had undoubtedly been precipitated there chemically. It was corroded by acid; it was evidently siliceous chalk similar in every respect to terrestrial chalk. It was cut through horizontally and transversally; by this means a veritable mummy—admirably preserved, although a trifle carbonized in places—was successfully laid bare.

The feet, which were very small, could only be extracted in a badly damaged state. The head came out very nearly intact: devoid of hair; skin glossy and crumpled, having passed into a leathery state; brain-cavity triangular in shape; singularly hatchet-faced, with a sort of trunk emerging almost from the forehead instead of a nose; a very small mouth with only a few teeth; two orbital holes, from which the eyes had doubtless been extracted, since the cavities were full of calcareous concretions. The arms were very long, hanging down beyond the thighs, the hands five-fingered, of which the fourth was much shorter than the others. The general appearance was slender. The skin, slightly charred all over, had undoubtedly been reddish-yellow.

A cast is being made of this singular inhabitant of another world, and we shall soon be able to send drawings.

He had nothing with him—no weapon, no ornamental object. The only other thing that was found in the fossilized space was a little metal disk covered in silver sulfate, with several lines deeply engraved in its surface.

It was impossible for the excavators to doubt that they had before their eyes a creature analogous to earthly humans, which had come from space in an extremely remote era, since the aerolith must have fallen in a very ancient geological period. But where had this planetary man come from? It could not be seriously imagined that he had come from the Moon. Aeroliths arrive with a velocity that precludes a lunar origin.

The discussion had already been going on for some time when Mr. Murchison, on examining the lines that furrowed the inner surface of the metal plate—which had finally been descaled—recognized a very clear depiction of a kind of rhinoceros, then one of a palm-tree, and, far away in the opposite corner, a neat representation of a star, similar to the Sun as drawn by a child.

The metal, which had been blackened by chemical reactions, was examined more closely; on cleaning it, the commission discovered another, smaller star beside the one that seemed to represent the Sun. Then they found another, more distant, then a third, and, finally, more distant still, a globe drawn much larger than the Sun. On measuring the distances between them, they were found to be manifestly in proportion to those separating the planets Mercury, Venus, the Earth and Mars from the Sun.

This was an indication entirely adequate to clarify the question. Was it not permissible to conclude, in fact, that the animal of which a specimen had been found under such strange circumstances knew the planets and was in consequence a thinking being, and therefore a man? Did not the entirely honorific size granted to the planet Mars, to the detriment of the others, demonstrate the pride of an inhabitant, and, at the same time, the mental limitation of the interplanetary human species?

In all probability, therefore, the aerolith must have originated from the planet Mars—which is, moreover, our nearest neighbor. We may consider it beyond doubt

24

that the planets really are inhabited, and that there are creatures thereon very similar to those on Earth.

Scientifically, of course, it is the environment that seems to determine the species. Mars has very nearly the same biological conditions as Earth; oceans, continents and mountains of ice can be seen there.[5] There is therefore, nothing so admissible in principle than to suspect the presence there of humans closely analogous to ourselves. If the type that has just been discovered is slightly different, it is necessary to remember that, biologically, Mars is more advanced than the Earth; that the aerolith fell thousands of years ago; and that its inhabitants in that period in its life might have been different from the present earthly species. It is unnecessary to deduce from this that Mars has never had, or does not presently have, inhabitants exactly similar to those of Earth.

How did the aerolith come to Earth, though, and how did it get away from the gravitational field of Mars? There are many points that are difficult to understand and must be submitted to modern scientific research. The aerolith brought with it a portion of ground, containing what is undoubtedly a tomb—which permits us to know how the dead are buried on that planet. A hole of the appropriate size is simply hollowed out in granite and the body is preserved by fossilizing it, with the aid of a bath loaded with calcium salts, just as your Saint-Allyre fountain near Clermont does with objects plunged into its waters; the corpse metamorphoses into calcareous stone.

---

[5] The famous Martian "canali" (channels) had yet to be "discovered" in 1864, so there is no mention of them in the account of the planet given here.

Yet another step has been taken in science—and what a step! A quarter of a century ago, people refused to believe in stones that fell from the sky. The French Académie, the English Royal Society and its German equivalent would not have conceded the point unless their members had been struck down on the spot by aeroliths! What will they say, now that an entire human being, perfectly preserved, has fallen to Earth from Mars, coming in person to reveal to us the admirable harmony that presides over the evolution of worlds!

The promised drawings will follow soon.

LETTER II

In which the names of the two Americans promise to become immortal. Is it a hoax or a reality? The opinions of two rival newspapers. Gossip at Independence and Leavenworth. How human industry profits from everything. At the foot of the Cordillera. Gifts and patronesses. Academies. What should we think about the mummy? How we can be sure that it has come from Mars. Its portrait. Singular appearances. A logogriph to decipher.

Although you have doubtless obtained further details of the James Peak aerolith from the English newspapers, I am sending you more accurate details in the present document.

What are they saying in France about the Paxton/Davis discovery? The public is still talking about it here. I got here, not without difficulty, on Saturday evening, and I can verify everything that I wrote to you from Richmond.

If we were not at war, and the journey not so long, the situation in Leavenworth—the last station on the route—would no longer be tenable. People are already arguing over food-supplies and guides. In order to deter unwelcome intruders, John Paxton had the fortunate idea of having reports inserted in the two rival newspapers of Springfield and Saint-Louis that everything that had been said was a crude and ridiculous fabrication made up by the local people in order to sell their foodstuffs and liquor at a better price—but the curiosity-seekers have not fallen into the trap. All the people that have not been deterred by fatigue and the enemy are heading in this direction. At Fort Mann I saw several officers arrested, the importance of the discovery having drawn them as far as the enemy lines.

The most direct route is to abandon the Missouri at Independence or Leavenworth and go upstream in a canoe as far as the first rapids on the Blue River, whose source is in the Cordillera; it is then necessary to continue on mule-back as far as Fort Mann, where the authorities were kind enough to put the commandant's boat at our disposal. Two further days on the Arkansas River suffices to reach Fort Bentz. There the Arkansas ceases to be navigable and it is necessary to go on into the mountains amid forests and crags. James Peak is more than three thousand meters high. It is an upsurge through the new red sandstone of the Jurassic stratum and an injection of crystalline rock. The Paxtons' mine is situated on the carboniferous terrain at the point of contact with porphyroid rocks. It is there that the aerolith was found. The fall appears to have occurred before the upsurge of the Cordillera; it is inclined at exactly the same angle as the neighboring strata.

When I saw it, the other day, for the first time, from a distance, it gave the initial impression of an enormous ball blackened by fire. It has been almost entirely excavated from the surrounding rock; it stands out in relief as if mounted in the soil. A wide trench has been dug all around it, but the trees and plants have been left in place, confusedly interlaced between the forest and the excavation, making the volcanic tint of the bolide stand out even more. It is cracked and pitted all over; sometimes the facets, polished like mirrors, reflect the rays of the Sun and dazzle you.

About a quarter of the surrounding ground has been left unexcavated, forming a sort of service-bridge for the works. At the center, the shaft has been dug; it is about

12 meters deep, two meters broad at the opening and 1.25 meters at the base. I have not been able to go down as yet, however, because the work is now proceeding very actively. It has been decided that the mass will be pierced completely through, and that gunpowder will then be exploded at strategic points to complete the exploration.

The Saint Louis Academy of Sciences has displayed a creditworthy enthusiasm. It has unanimously voted an allocation of $2000 to carry out research. Would your Académie des Sciences have shown such zeal and generosity? The inhabitants of Leavenworth, Batesville, Karkabia and Indianapolis having made a subscription, the Paxtons have already received $1000 from people who want to participate, according to their resources, in the communal task. By way of compensation, Mr. Paxton has sent his patronesses necklaces and cups made from the stone of the bolide.

Specimens of the mass are, moreover, beginning to be sold at a very high price, along with crude figurines depicting the mummy fund in the middle of the aerolith. One of them was offered to me for four dollars as I passed through Indianapolis. It is a source of unexpected wealth for the workmen and the inhabitants of the interior. Little wooden shacks are being erected along the road between Fort Bentz and the excavation, and the track through the James Forest is being enlarged.

Evidently, people will come here in summer as your Parisians go to Biarritz, Ems and Baden. I have already encountered a group of tourists from Saint Louis on the far side of the Arkansas rapids, partly composed of women, and the most elegant in the city. I recognized the famous Mrs. Howard, with whose history you are no doubt familiar. She played a considerable role in the last campaign. Taken prisoner by two of Grant's officers, she seduced the senior aide-de-camp; two duels followed, and she ended up bringing the federal cavalry's commanding officer back to Lee's camp, enchained by her beauty. She has been living in Saint Louis since the winter.

The Paxtons' operation is not very large. Situated on the western side of the mountain, a long way from the nearest town, it was almost unknown before now, except to officers from Fort Bentz who sometimes extended their patrols this far. The entire property consists of two large buildings connected by a central unit, a few wooden storehouses, blackened by intemperate weather, a farmhouse and, some distance away, the hangars designed to house the carboniferous shale and the workmen's cabins. At present, Mr. Paxton is having a large wooden house analogous to the haciendas of South America built for visitors.

The scientific commission is already numerous. The left wing of the main building has been reserved for them. We are still awaiting two of our most highly-qualified zoologists from Philadelphia and Richmond, Mr. Wintow and Mr. Ziegler. They have been delayed in Petersburg, but a letter that arrived this morning notified us of their imminent arrival. Mr. Murchison, who was present at the moment of the discovery, has agreed to take the responsibility of supervising the research, with Mr. Davis.

A hole about one and a half meters in diameter is being hollowed out with picks. The rock is still porphyroid, very similar in appearance to ejections of the same sort that come to light in the midst of our metamorphic shales, in which crystals are found in abundance. Every workman who brings back anything curious or exposes the remains of an object receives a reward of two dollars. They are under orders to proceed very gently and cautiously.

At the level of the metal plate that covered the calcareous tomb, several more little rods about 50 centimeters long have been found, apparently made of the same alloy as the amphora. Mr. Sawton, professor of chemistry at Indianapolis, arrived recently, so the precise analyses carried out by Mr. Davis can be checked.

The interplanetary man, or animal, has been deposited in Mr. Paxton's mineralogical collection. He has been placed horizontally, in the position in which he was found in the bosom of the rocky mass. Mr. Davis did not want anyone to touch him or to strip off his covering before the scientists were able to examine him at their leisure; he still remains in his sepulcher.

No cast has yet been made, as I promised you, but photographs have been taken and drawings made. With these lines I am sending you a large drawing of the aerolith that I made on site and sketch of the inhabitant of Mars—if that really is where the individual in question has come from. It is no more than a rough drawing taken from my notebook; it is however, exact enough for your engraver to make copies of it. You will almost recognize the portrait that I have made for you.

It seems as if one is confronted by one of those old sepulchers that ornament the chapels of basilicas. The calcareous concretions stand in for the sculpture, and the mummy itself for the statue. The mass of siliceous calcium carbonate in which the singular individual is enclosed is quadrangular in shape. It measures very nearly two meters in length by 75 centimeters in breadth and 50 centimeters in height. About a third of the limestone has been cut transversally to enable the mummy to be better observed, in such a way that one can detach the block or replace it in its original position at will. A large portion of the covering has been removed in places, which permits the mummy's true form to be discerned.

It seems at first glance that one is confronted by a large monkey 1,35 meters tall, lying down at full extent, and half-covered in chalk. It is only on making a more detailed examination that this impression is overcome. There is, in fact, nothing as strange as the face, which is at one and the same time that of a monkey, a human being and an elephant.

Take a human head; strike the back of the skull with a laundry-beater until it is flattened out, so as to present a surface some 30 centimeters across; then continue flattening the two cheeks obliquely. You will have a plane behind, two triangular faces at the sides; that is the exact conformation of the head. From the top of this sort of triangular blade hangs a trunk, broad in the upper part and narrow in the lower; it has been badly damaged, but its diameter varies between 15 centimeters and four or five. It half-covers up a tiny mouth with very thick lips, somewhat reminiscent of the muzzle of a rodent in its smallness, with three teeth in the lower jaw and two in the upper. Below that, a receding chin and a very long neck; narrow shoulders; arms 80 centimeters long; hands 30 centimeters; fingers narrow and pointed, the fourth shorter than the others.

It was in error that I said the feet were short; they are longer than the hands and rather narrow.

The skull is devoid of hair, but that signifies nothing, because it is slightly charred. The breast is hairy—or, at least, a few grey or reddish hairs are perceptible within the covering. In the places where the skin has not been decomposed by heat, it is brown with a red tint.

The large plate that was covering the tomb is very curious. The metal of which it is composed has not yet been analyzed; it has the appearance of silver blackened by acid. Its entire surface is granular and contains pockets of gas. The side that was facing the tomb is smoother and a large quantity of lines can be made out upon it, which remain to be studied: designs of fantastic animals and bizarre objects.

In one corner, close to a sort of rhinoceros, the stars I mentioned previously can be seen quite clearly. Whether by chance or not, they can certainly be taken for the Sun, Venus, Earth and Mars, at their respective distances—then further away, Jupiter and Saturn, with discrepancies in the distances as they are presently measured.

In the depiction, Mars has a diameter of three centimeters, the Sun and Mercury each have a diameter of one centimeter, Venus and Earth half a centimeter, Jupiter and Saturn two centimeters. Above them, slightly effaced, tightly-packed signs are visible, which might well represent numbers—but I should not anticipate at present. The commission is due to begin its discussions tomorrow; I shall leave all responsibility to its members.

At the top of the plate, to the left, beneath a sort of palm tree, Mr. Davis pointed out several designs to me, which seem to represent human beings exactly analogous to the one that has fallen to Earth; it is undoubtedly this plate that will permit us to clarify the mystery, if it can be clarified.

I am sending you these lines in haste. I shall send you an account of the discussions taking place here by the next post.

LETTER III

At Paxton House. A commission of scientists. Poor pho-
tographs of Messrs. Newbold and Greenwight. Speak up,
Mr. President! A great geologist. A great astronomer.
Mr. Greenwight on Le Verrier's planet. The editor's in-
fluence on the author. William Seringuier and advertis-
ing. Biétry shawls and Oléine. Mr. Stek (of the Institute).

The commission was conclusively constituted on
Thursday and the discussion began the following day.
The rumor has reached us that Lyell, the English geologist, has crossed the Atlantic, sent by the London Geological Society.[6] No official notification has been given
to us of this voyage, and as it is impossible to keep those
scientists who have been here for more than a fortnight
waiting indefinitely in expectation of further arrivals, it
has been unanimously decided that we should set to
work without further delay.

The meeting-hall is in the main wing of Mr. Paxton's house; it is capable of accommodating about 100
people. The mummy, in its calcareous shroud, has been
placed at the center, along with the metal rods and the

---

[6] Charles Lyell (1797-1875) had recently published *The An-*
tiquity of Man (1863), the latest in a series of works that
played a central role in establishing a "uniformitarian" geology, which took it as proven that the Earth and its natural species were very ancient, the surface of the Earth and its inhabitant species having evolved very slowly. His work was one of
the foundation-stones on which Darwin's theory of the origin
of species by natural selection rested. Had he ever arrived at
Paxton House, the discussions there would certainly have become more contentious.

amphorae; the metal plate has been set up facing the widow, in the daylight. Chairs and stools are ranged around, then benches made for the occasion—for seats are scarce in Paxton House. Mr. Paxton has had a sort of platform built for the conference table, facing the entrance door. Below that a long table has been set, clad in sacramental green serge, for the secretaries. Finally, at the back, facing the conference-table and behind the commission's seats, Mr. Paxton has been accommodating enough to reserve an enclosure for the journalists; there are representatives here from both the Northern and Southern press, including Washington, Philadelphia and Boston. We are all living, almost in perfect harmony, under the flag of science.

Here are the names of the commissioners. You will recognize several famous names among them. I shall list them as I see them, grouped before me.

At the conference-table, occupying the presidential armchair, Monsieur Newbold, perhaps the southern geologist who has given most service to science: a man of about 60 years of age, educated in the school of Buch, Humboldt, etc.,[7] who has only one fault so far as we are concerned, which it is that he speaks too softly. Profound physiognomy, bright eyes, almost always leans both his elbows on the table with his hands joined together in front of his nose. All in all, an excellent president, accustomed to the use of the hand-bell.

---

[7] Leopold von Buch (1771-1853) and Alexander von Humboldt (1769-1859) were German scientists, the former a noted geologist and he latter a philosophically-inclined naturalist whose *Kosmos* was a significant attempt to offer a comprehensive physical description of the world as it was understood by science in the early 19th century.

To his right, the vice-president, Mr. Greenwight, Philadelphia's most noted astronomer. Tall, blond, energetic, well-built. Yankee in appearance and in fact. His reputation is long-established. Graduated from the Military School in New York, he initially devoted himself to chemistry, studying oxygenated water, but was suddenly seized by a lively infatuation for astronomy. Called by circumstance to Philadelphia, he discovered two minor planets and, after an interval of several days, rediscovered Monsieur Le Verrier's famous planet Neptune.[8] He is honest and loyal by nature, in spite of being a Yankee; on the day when the French newspapers told him that his planet had already been discovered by a Parisian astronomer he ran straight to the Academy and made the following speech, which brought forth many wry smiles:

"Gentlemen, let no one be mistaken; Le Verrier, without a telescope and solely by mans of calculation, was the first to discover the star that I observed on September 27. It is unique; it is marvelous; Le Verrier is henceforth the Columbus of the Heavens. As for me,

---

[8] Urbain Le Verrier (1811-1877) is universally credited as the discoverer of Neptune, having calculated its ostensible position in 1846 from observed discrepancies in Neptune's orbit; the British astronomer John Couch Adams performed a similar calculation almost simultaneously, but got it slightly wrong. Johann Galle and Heinrich d'Arrest of the Berlin Observatory were the first people actually to observe the planet by means of a telescope, a few days after Le Verrier's calculation told them where to look. Le Verrier went on to "discover" the planet Vulcan by calculations based on perturbations of Mercury's orbit; numerous astronomers "confirmed" his determination with false sightings, but the "discovery," like many other errors of the era, was subsequently effaced from the reference books.

gentleman, I shall forever be their Amerigo Vespucci. It is necessary to render unto Caesar that which is Caesar's."

No one in Philadelphia has forgotten, however, that if Monsieur Le Verrier had been ill for a few days, or if he had made an arithmetical error, the honor of the great discovery would have reverted to America. On such threads do honors depend!

Mr. Greenwight speaks well. His voice is powerful and vigorous, but sometimes too rich in *heu-heu*—the sort of noise that is formed by the fusion of two mangled words. Nevertheless he is an orator, and an orator who occupies a high rank in our political assemblies to boot. Very highly regarded in Philadelphia, he is evidently one of those who, in Paris, would be awarded the Grand Cross of the Legion of Honor.

To the president's left are seated Messrs. Wintow and Rink, a zoologist and an ethnologist.

Mr. Wintow is the most peculiar little man that one could ever see: a professor at Washington, decorated in Russia, Italy and Spain, he does not seem any less discontented and grumpy. He is a naturalized American, for he was English by birth. He has occupied the chair of zoology at Washington for more than 20 years; I believe that he is the doyen of zoologists. Well in with all the authorities and the Church, he has covered America with little two-shilling pamphlets and large volumes at four or even five dollars, issued by Nossamm and Sons, the official publisher of the city's Medical School. He is well-known to the students as their examiner. He is a member of the Academy of Philadelphia and an honorary member of the French Institut. He is a successful man, and it only remains for him to make a success of his son Alphonse.

Mr. Rink is taller by some decimeters than his illustrious colleague Mr. Wintow; he is, however, of lesser stature in the opinion of provincial academies. His speech is fluent, but prickly and grating. He has professed himself to be an anthropologist for a number of years, and no one complains of it, least of all those who occupy themselves with political economics. He writes for the *New Review* and holds court with journalists. He can be conveniently bracketed with William Seringuier, who sits a few places away from me; that name will doubtless have aggravated your nerves more than once; one sees his advertisements all over the place, like those in France for Biétry shawls[9] and Olein,[10] for catching fish more rapidly.

William Seringuier has ended up, thanks to advertising, on the staff of Hacken & Co. in New York, certainly the most powerful publisher in America. Thanks primarily to the stupidity of some of his colleagues, he ended up making a reputation for himself among the broader public of merchants, easily enticed by engravings and overblown words. He is welcomed in Mr. Rink's home, and Mr. Rink returns his visits.

---

[9] M. Biétry was a textile manufacturer who became famous for mass-producing Cashmere shawls; his wares were exhibited at the great exhibitions of the mid-19th century, including the *Exposition Universelle* to which Parville provided one of the guide-books.

[10] Olein (*Oléine* in French), a derivative of fats that was one of the first compounds isolated and exploited by the burgeoning science and technology of organic chemistry, was indeed marketed at one time as an aid in angling, allegedly attracting fish by means of its odorant qualities. It has many other uses, which have long overtaken that one.

Mr. Rink is universally reckoned to be a man of the world and an excellent naturalist. The president, Mr. Newbold, sometimes looks at him from the corner of his eye between his joined fingers. Mr. Newbold, in fact, has never wanted to hear talk of fossil humans; that is why he has hastened to see the inhabitant of the planet Mars—and Mr. Rink is the most energetic and most high-profile defender, after Mr. Shafford,[11] of human fossils. Here, as with you, our scientists are not always in accord.

Further to the left, at the end of the platform, sits a little grey man—grey from head to toe—admirably shaven, not much taller than the man from Mars, but better turned-out. He is the permanent secretary of the Boston Agricultural Society, here serving as assistant secretary, an agronomist-cum-chemist and businessman. There is something slightly Mephistophelean in his expression and his smile. He is, it is said, the author—in collaboration with a famous poet—of a treatise on *Coprolites* [12] that created a certain stir in its time.

Below the platform, more or less comfortably seated before the green serge, are two of our old ac-

---

[11] Although Mr. Shafford is not a character in the story, he appears to be fictitious, and the reference to him is therefore a trifle gnomic.

[12] Coprolites are pieces of fossilized dung; they are much prized by palaeontologists for the information they can yield regarding the diets of prehistoric animals. The term coprology, given to this scientific endeavour, is also sometimes used sarcastically, to describe the study of dirty books; that is presumably why Parville mentions the mysterious grey man's collaboration with a famous poet. We never do discover his name, and he never gets to play the role of Devil's Advocate that is seemingly reserved for him here.

quaintances, Mr. Paxton and Mr. Davis, and a third scientist, whom it is a pleasure for me to introduce to you,
Mr. Stek. You will know him by reputation. He is an
astronomer, journalist, naturalist, officer, bibliophile,
poet, scholar, Hellenist, meteorologist, geologist, chemist, physician, professor, examiner, engineer, columnist,
milliner...and I shall stop there. A great friend of disorder, it is to him that we owe the paradox: "Disorder is
order." He is about 70 years old. He is slightly reminiscent of Quasimodo—your Quasimodo—and yet he is
handsome. He has something of Dante in his expression,
something of Byron in his gait; his spine is exceedingly
bent, but he seems tall and proud. He has a mottled face,
but I know that he conjures up dreams of Romantic
characters. His hair is grey-brown, turning into the
Milky Way; it floats in the wind and shelters his deep-set
eyes; he never dyes it, for disorder is order—and yet
again, public opinion deems him right. He does not always keep his eyes open. When he is composing a cou-
plet, he half-closes them. If it is a matter of an interplanetary calculation, he closes them entirely. Have a
chat with him—for he excels in the art of conversation—
and he opens and closes them alternately to mark the
rhythm of his discourse. If he had enemies—he never
has had any—he would most certainly keep them wide
open.

Stek holds back or lets fly according to circumstances. He never speaks ill of his colleagues in science
or journalism, but he thinks it nevertheless. How many
times have we caught him laughing, in a wicked fashion,
at the errors or satires of others, then writing the following day that the book he was reading was interesting
and will sell two thousand copies? If I did not know that
he was born in Petersburg I would take him for a Nor-

man, a true Norman! He has very slender fingers and a philosophical grip. Confusion is impossible.

Stek has done good work, but he would have been able to do better. He is too much of a butterfly; he is more an artistic scientist than a scientific artist. The two sides of his character collide with one another and hinder one another. He dresses badly, and that pains the Academy of Philadelphia, which is very strong on etiquette. His trousers are too short, allowing a glimpse of underclothes that are too long; his shirt is loosely agape, within a waistcoat innocent of buttons, and his tie describes an elongated trajectory around his neck, displaying its slack knot from sunrise to sunset. All too frequently, a handkerchief hangs out of his pocket, floating like a national flag from a mizzen mast. His olive frock-coat is as old as its owner, but its flaps bulge out before and behind as if to protect Stek from contact with the multitude. How many people would pay dear for that frock-coat, which is the despair of the Academicians of Philadelphia?

Stek is a true eccentric. Knock at his door: if he is in a good mood, he will let you in; if he got out of bed on the wrong side, he will say: "I'm not here, sir; come back in an hour"—and he will slam the door in your face.

Come back at the end of an hour. "Is Mr. Stek there?"

Stek opens and closes his eyes twice. He takes out his watch and looks at it as if he were looking at something nebulous. "That's right," he says, "it's time; come in, sir."

"Come in" is an easy thing to say, but is not as easy to do as one might think. Stek takes a stride, hops, slides, turns and advances, but the visitor remains where he is.

A corridor is before him. To the right and the left, piles of books mount up to the ceiling, disposed like the two sides of a railway embankment. It is necessary to go into this cutting: blockades and rocks, composed of brochures and old books agglutinated by dust, impede the passage; an old forgotten measuring instrument bars the way like a headland. Light is scarcely admitted into this sanctuary.

"Come on, get a move on, sir!" cries Stek, sniggering. "We'll never get there."

The visitor, thus encouraged, launches himself forwards—and, after a few false steps and a few stumbles, succeeds in reaching the first room. The same aspect: tunnels of books, walls of pamphlets and memoirs. Stek does not pause for breath. He disappears behind another embankment of print. It is necessary to follow, at all costs. The corner is turned.

"We're here," says Stek, fidgeting in that dust like a tardigrade in a gutter.[13]

Where the devil is he? you think, searching for him in an enormous room garnished throughout with bizarre stalactites and stalagmites of books. A little noise, reminiscent of that of a hedgehog passing through the undergrowth, puts you on the track. Stek is already sitting under a triumphal arch of volumes belonging to all the libraries in the world, with a fireplace behind him—empty in summer, with a log fire in winter—at a little table

---

[13] Tardigrades, in this meaning, are small arachnid mites familiarly known as "water-bears". They were among the most commonly-cited "infusoria," a general term then given to creatures only visible by means of early 19th century microscopes.

with an inkwell, a pencil and paper. To one side is a snuff-box and a cigar-butt, with its ash still in place.

"Sit down, sir, and we'll have a chat."

The visitor searches for a chair. His gaze does not encounter any.

"Moments are precious, sir. How can I be of service to you? Sit down."

Four dusty antiquarian books display their nudity in front of the hearth;[14] the visitor perches on them grate-fully. "I have invented," he says, "a means of steering balloons, and I've come to ask for your advice. I took a mouse and hitched it to a little toy roundabout. At the hub of the wheel I arranged four little wings into a pro-peller, as in a windmill, and I saw these winglets screw themselves up into the air, transporting my roundabout and my mouse. As the mouse became frantic with fright and turned faster and faster, the roundabout and its wings flew higher and higher; I soon lost sight of them."

"Sir," says Stek, "your winglets would bear away an elephant even more effectively. You and your mouse have solved the great problem of directing balloons. It's now no more than a question of technology; the scien-tific solution is found. Sit down again."

"I think so, Mr. Stek, but, a few minutes afterwards, as I went in search of another mouse and another round-about to repeat the experiment, I heard a loud whistling noise; a little black mass fell a few meters away from me, and I had no difficulty recognizing my first mouse and my first roundabout. The mouse was dead and the winglets in pieces."

---

[14] Old books, in the mid-19th century, were quite likely to be unbound; publishers had only recently begun binding them as a matter of course.

"Time is precious, sir, and life is short. Your system is extremely ingenious, and I tell you that you could lift an elephant with it. Don't worry about the rest. It's a technological question. It's no longer a matter for scientists, but for technologists and workmen. Persist in your work and come back to seek my advice when you have succeeded."

The visitor withdraws, enlightened with respect to his system, and makes his way forward as best he can, guided by his host and perfectly convinced that disorder is order. That's Stek.

I forgot to say that he only receives visitors on Sundays. He was won great renown by means his originality, and there is no more popular man in America. If someone says to someone else, "Stek will be here imminently," you can be sure of finding them waiting patiently several hours later.

I do not know whether I should pass in review over the whole audience; I fear that I might bore you. It might be better to select a few more of the most notable and most loquacious among them, in order that you will be able to follow the debate. All the other members are arranged around and in front of the conference-table, including Mr. Haughton, professor of paleontology at Boston; Mr. Liesse, professor of geology at Albany; Mr. Saunter, director of the Nashville Institute; Mr. Ziegler, president of the Richmond Academy; Mr. Sawton, holder of the chair of chemistry at Indianapolis; Mr. Murchison, member of the geological section of the Washington Institute; Mr. Oupeau, the chief of medicine at Baltimore Hospital; Messrs. Skrimpton, Liess, White, Millon and Karter of the Academy of Saint Louis; Mr. Owerght, professor of astrophysics at Richmond; Mr. Sawen, engineer and chief of naval construction at Annapolis; Mr. G. Mitchell, highly distinguished anatomist of Frankfurt; Messrs. Saunters, Cayley, Merit and Bug, artillery officers; Mr. Sieman, professor of chemistry and quantitative analysis at the Washington Mining School; Mr. Logan, assistant astronomer at Petersburg; Mr. O'Clintock, examiner in physics at the Mining School; Mr. Larrab, editor of the *Washington Journal of Agriculture*; Mr. Richardson, engineer in the establishment of Filox & Son; Mr. Engelhard, professor of cosmography at Springfield; Monsieur l'Abbé Amaurose, a French missionary resident in Nashville for ten years; Mr. Gouge, member of the London Geological Society; Mr. Evans, professor of mathematics at Indianapolis, and, finally, your most humble servant.

LETTER IV

Setting the scene. The following. The journalists. William Seringuier. Abbé Omnish. Williamson. On the difficult of beginning at the beginning. Discussion. The infinitely small and the infinitely large. Molecular astronomy. What matter is. The diabolical dance of all that surrounds us. Lilliputian stars. Two hundred and fifty thousand years to count how many stars might be enclosed in the head of a pin. The harmony of the universe.

We are numerous, as you see, and we still have behind us the correspondents of our principal newspapers. William Seringuier has made the trip, in spite of his legendary laziness. Abbé Omnish, incontrovertibly our premier popularizer of science, is at his post—as are A. Williamson, the pretentious writer for the Washington *Strand*, and Noirot de Sauw, a physician out of Molière,[15] resurrected in the 19th century.

A few more biographical comments, and I shall bring this overly long scene-setting to a conclusion.

I ought, in fact, to tell you that Haughton, whose name I put at the head of the list, passes for one of the leading paleontologists of our era. He is still quite young and, in stark contrast to Stek, never goes out without his stick in his hand and his hand in a well-tailored glove.

---

[15] The famous French dramatist was rather cynical about physicians, most notably in *Le médécin malgré lui* (1666), in which the woodcutter Signarelle impersonates a physician and achieves a not-very-remarkable "cure" by introducing a female patient's secret lover to her home in the guise of his apothecary.

His tight frame indicates a former military man; I believe that he once saw active service. He is very benevolent, it is said, or, at any rate, very indulgent, perhaps a little too devoted to rose-water in spite of his military bearing. He was the man who, while introducing one of the leaden works of William Seringuier to the Boston Academy two years ago, cried out in a moment of comic eloquence: "Finally, what more can I say to the Academy? The author, with his customary skill, has contrived to draw all the thorns out of science, to leave nothing but the roses."

The phrase has become historic, and, when anyone wants to point out Mr. Haughton, they never fail to say "the paleontologist of the thorn-less roses". It is a fact that Mr. Haughton is a gentleman in every sense of the word.

Who else should I describe for you? Liesse, the Albany professor and mining engineer, elected two years ago to the Academy is tall and thin. He has done a lot of work on metamorphism[16]—as has his colleague, the engineer Vanbrée, who, less fortunate than him, is still waiting for a chair. Liesse has made aeroliths his academic specialism; he was one of the first to get here. Oupeau, a physician from Baltimore, is recognizable in every country in the world by his white cravat, which rises up above his ears, and the stiffness of his torso. He is not an orator, it must be said. Owerght, professor of astrophysics at Richmond, is a friend of the astronomer Greenwight and a fine mathematician.

I should stop there; I'll never get to the end of the list, and my paper is visible shrinking. I shall offer fur-

---

[16] The study of changes in the constitution of rocks resulting from pressure, heat, chemical action, etc.

ther descriptions, if the opportunity arises, as the discussion continues.

It was on Thursday June 22 that the commission held its first session—and what a session it was! Opened at 1 p.m., it did not close until 7 p.m.. All that I got out of it is one fact perfectly demonstrated: that there is nothing so difficult as to begin at the beginning. That was the matter of determining who should speak and how the progress of the discussion should be regulated. Newbold covered himself in sweat with the effort of ringing his hand-bell, and his hands came together and separated again like the crank-shaft of a steam-engine.

Should we begin by discussing the possibility of celestial bodies falling to Earth?—a primarily astronomical question, on which Greenwight was particularly insistent. Should we not first devote ourselves, on the contrary, to the examination of the mummy from the viewpoint of physics or physiology? Would it not be preferable to examine the subject from the viewpoint of chemistry? And the hand-bell rings, and Messrs Wintow and Rink raise their voices; Messrs. Sawton, Davis and Murchison thump their fists on the green serge; Mr. Stek closes his eyes; Newbold tries to speak; William Seringuier shouts at the top of his voice that Newbold has no common sense, and that, if he were doing his job, silence would soon be re-established. What a racket! You would scarcely get an idea of it by recalling the heyday of your parliamentary debates.

Eventually, Greenwight ends up claiming the floor.

"Gentlemen," he says, "it seems to me that the debate is going astray and that neither astronomy, nor anthropology, nor physiology should take the first step. Everything should be taken in order. Now, first of all, what are we dealing with? An aerolith. So, the floor reverts by right and in fact to geologists and chemists. Once that point is clarified, I think that it will be appropriate to see from what sector of the sky this mass has come to us, if it is not of terrestrial origin; that will be the concern of the astronomers and physicists; finally, it will be the turn of the physiologists, paleontologists, etc. Hazard, moreover, gentlemen, has shown us the way. Have we not chosen a geologist as our president, an astronomer as vice-president and a zoologist and an anthropologist as secretaries?"

"Mr. Greenwight seems to me to be right," says Newbold, "and if the commission has no objection to it, I shall set the day's agenda thus: geological discussion; astronomical discussion; anthropological discussion."

No one demands to speak.

There is a prolonged ring of the hand-bell. "The resolution is adopted," murmurs the president, and puts his hands together.

The floor is given to Mr. Paxton first, and then to Mr. Davis. They recount in full detail the various incidents in the discovery of the aerolith, which you already know.

Mr. Davis then reports the analyses that he has made of the bolide's surface. Mr. Paxton, who has repeated them, reports his own findings. The agreement is almost perfect.

Mr. Sieman, professor of quantitative analysis at the Mining School, short, mocking and extremely skeptical: "Can Mr. Sawton tell me whether he is perfectly sure that the presence of cesium has been established? The analysis reports traces. How was it carried out? I beg pardon for insisting, but the commission will perhaps recall that I have already fund cesium, two years ago, in several mineral species: aphanite, nickelocher, triphylite, panabase and bournonite,[17] and this matter is therefore of direct interest to me."

Mr. Sawton: "I simply used a spectroscope, and the characteristic ray was present in the spectra of almost all the specimens placed in the flame."

Mr. Sieman: "You did not find any substance foreign to the Earth?"

Mr. Sawton: "No."

Mr. Davis: "I should add that certain crystals, those of silver, for example, do not have the same form that they do here. I found crystalline silver that was no longer in the octahedral form but organized in prismatic squares."

The President: "Mr. Davis saw the bolide when it was still enclosed in the ground. Were the strata horizontal?"

---

[17] Parville inserts three footnotes into this list, defining aphanite and nickelocher as minerals containing arsenic, the former in combination with copper and the latter with nickel, triphylite as a mineral composed of phosphorus in combination with iron and manganese, and panabase and bournonite as combinations of sulphur with antimony and copper. More recent terminology uses aphanite as a general description of any kind of rock so closely-textured that its grains are invisible to the naked eye and has replaced "nickelocher" with the name annabergite. Triphylite was subsequently identified as a composite of lithium and iron phosphates with traces of manganese. "Panabase" also became obsolete in the meaning Parville cites, being replaced by tetrahedrite; as well as copper and antimony sulfides, it usually contains traces of other metals. Bournonite is a composite of antimony, lead and copper sulfides. The modern descriptions I have consulted do not report any traces of cesium in any of these minerals.

Mr. Davis: "No, Mr. President; inclined about thirty-three degrees north-west. For me, there is not the slightest doubt that the aerolith fell in a remote geological epoch, for almost exactly the same inclination was observable in its principal axis. It was most certainly in place when the Cordillera lifted up the neighboring strata as it was elevated."

Mr. Newbold: "I should point out to Mr. Davis that above the carboniferous layer there is a deposit varying in depth by between one and three meters. That deposit is not diluvian, and on a map that I drew myself—not for this circumstance, of course—it is designated as *loose* or *landslide terrain*. It comes from the soil of virgin forests. Is it that layer whose inclination Mr. Davis has measured? If so, the datum is worthless."

Mr. Davis: "That layer had been stripped away then I arrived, and I could, of course, only make my initial measurements on the ancient deposits."

Mr. Wintow: "You did not recognize any trace of human bones in that superior layer, or any worked flint?"

Mr. Paxton: "In an excavation a little further away to the north-west, I found a mass of stone arrow-heads and what I believe to be aurochs bones—but the arrow-heads were porphyry, not flint."

Mr. Rink: "I should like to see these objects, Mr. Paxton. The Institut de France is very interested in these questions. Monsieur de Quatrefages [18] will be delighted if we send him a few specimens. Mr. Lyell, for his part, will receive with interest any details that you care to give him."

---

[18] Jean-Louis-Armand de Quatrefages de Bréau (1810-1892), a noted naturalist and physical anthropologist.

The President: "Gentlemen, our sessions are over-burdened. Permit me to bring you back to the question. The first point to elucidate is this: is the rocky mass discovered by Mr. Paxton really an aerolith? I think that no one is in doubt that its composition and position in the strata seem to prove that it is. For myself, I do not think that any other rock presenting its specific characteristics has ever been found on Earth."

Mr. Haughton: "The geologist of the thorns supports the opinion of the President as to the evidence."

Mr. Liesse, the mining engineer, asks to make an observation. "I think," he says, "that an authentic bolide has indeed been exposed—but, in order to put our conclusion beyond the shadow of a doubt, it appears to me to be important to see whether any other rocks analogous to it in composition can be found in the vicinity in the same rock-formation. Might we not hypothesize, in fact, that it was produced in a certain epoch of concretion, or in a rain of materials of a composition identical to that of the aerolith? We have examples of geodes or crystallizations that are completely different, in substantial composition, from the surrounding terrain."

Mr. Rink: "We can only gain from doing what Mr. Liesse asks, but, in my view, the question is settled. The thick black glaze that surrounds the mass indicates traces of fusion, and the rock can only have been cracked in consequence of a long passage through the atmosphere at an enormous velocity. Its origin is therefore extraterrestrial."

The President: "I shall put the proposition to the vote. Will those in favor of adopting it raise their hands."

A large number of hands go up. The proposition is adopted.

Mr. Vanbrée: "I should like to make the observation to the commission that, although the opinion that it has just expressed does not imply anything about the true origin of the mummy, it is no less important from the point of view of planetary composition. It is a bolide, so it comes from space; its composition, therefore, is that of the celestial bodies; thus, according to the analyses carried out, the elements of other worlds must be very nearly those of the Earth; throughout our solar system we shall find the same rocks and the same metals, in different crystalline forms.

"This is, as everyone understands, a big step forward. If the constituent elements of worlds are the same, it is permissible to deduce that our entire solar system has a common origin. I do not insist; I only wish to draw the attention of geologists and astronomers to this point."

Mr. Murchison: "It is a pure and simple confirmation of the theories of Laplace,[19] which make our planet and the Sun the debris and fragments of a large primitive nebula."

Mr. Owerght: "Evidently, but whether we had found the same substances or whether we had found different ones, it would not be possible to conclude anything in consequence, for all matter is characterized by the grouping of its elements and the juxtaposition of its

---

[19] The cosmogonic theory devised by Pierre-Simon, Marquis de Laplace (1749-1827), elaborating theses initially put forward by René Descartes (1596-1650), dominated 19th century thought regarding the origin of our solar system, and solar systems in general; the theory advanced by Parville's Mr. Greenwight in the next chapter is a simplified and slightly modified version of it

molecules. Now, that juxtaposition depends on temperature, and on the rapidity with which changes in temperature occur. Thus, as the temperature of each heavenly body has varied abruptly or differently, there will be as many causes of transformations of matter, and as many origins of different substances."

Mr. O'Clintock. "I tend to agree with my honorable colleague's opinion. It appears to me to be quite certain, according to present scientific knowledge, that bodies only differ by virtue of their molecular grouping, as constellations of the heavens are distinguishable by the positioning of stars. Take any two or three cities; seen from a balloon at a great height, they scarcely differ, but a little closer to the ground, their appearance changes, solely because of the arrangement of houses and the topographical distribution of streets, promenades and edifices.

"Such is the case for a mineral or any other substance. Since natural forces will have placed the streets, promenades and houses of these little molecular cities in such and such a manner, you will get a different impression. Everything depends on the architect, in this case the influence of the predominant force."

Mr. Sieman: "I approve unreservedly of my savant colleagues' way of seeing, and, if the commission will authorize me to hold the floor for a few minutes..."

("Yes, yes!")

"...I will add that personal endeavors developing the view of American and foreign mathematicians permit me to advance the hypothesis that any body whatsoever represents, very exactly and in miniature, an entire stellar system like the one that we perceive in the sky every night: the Milky Way. The astronomers who are kind enough to be listening to me know better than I do that the Earth is a molecule among all those innumerable heavenly bodies, whose ensemble appears to our eyes as a long white streak.

"The Earth is an integral part of the Milky Way. Well, a body, whatever it might be—think, for the sake of focusing the mind, of wood, gold, or diamond—is nothing but a mass of variously-grouped molecular constellations. From the large to the small, the analogy is complete. Our eyes are not equipped to perceive the worlds in these infinitely tiny systems in every detail, but might not other animals better constituted than we are be able to perceive them? It is obvious that, if you could construct a microscope of sufficient power, you would succeed in magnifying the molecular worlds of each petty terrestrial Milky Way, as one magnifies and refines the nebulosity of the heavens with telescopes. Take a glance; you will then see what appears to be a confused mass arranged with an admirable symmetry.[20]

---

[20] This thesis is, in essence, a re-envisioning in the context of contemporary science of one of the central propositions of occult science: "as above, so below;" dozens of works had been written, in the wake of the revival of interest in occult science in the Renaissance, regarding presumed harmonic relationships between the (human or Earthly) microcosm and the stellar macrocosm. Their ambition and complexity were refueled rather than being made redundant by Copernican theory, and such mystical systems as Emmanuel Swedenborg's still made much of metaphorical resonances of that sort in the early 19th century. The substitution of an atomic/molecular microcosm for the human one was a natural consequence of the development of microscopy and the renewal of atomic theory by chemists. The analogy became even more appealing at the beginning of the 20th century, when a clearer discrimination had been made between molecules and atoms and a model of

"The bodies will be pierced by light; you will discover enormous interstices, empty spaces, like the interplanetary spaces. Then, from place to place, worlds harmoniously grouped, with atmospheres around each one, and—a marvelous spectacle!—all these little molecular worlds rotating with a vertiginous rapidity, describing more or less oblique trajectories, like the large worlds in the sky. Then, by further augmenting the power of your instrument, you will end up seeing other small worlds around each of these principal worlds, satellites like our Moon, carrying out their rotational movements majestically and regularly: the infinitely small is so infinitely large!

"All these movements are so rapid that they are ungraspable by human beings—but they are sufficient, nevertheless, to have an effect on us! And what strange effects! Heat and light, gentlemen—for whose true causes we did not know where to look for a long time, but which we have now discovered!

"These infinitely rapid movements impact upon us; they affect us. Directly? No. These little worlds are masses so tiny that they produce no more effect on us than the grains of sand that flew through the air at Voltaire's *Micromégas* [21]—but these little worlds, which swarm in cadence in their intermolecular medium, discover there an atmosphere whose mass is of the same order as they are; they agitate that atmosphere; they give

---

the atom was proposed that represented it as a positively-charged nucleus orbited by "planetary" electrons.

[21] *Micromégas* (1752) is a satirical *conte philosophique* in which Earth is visited by a giant inhabitant of the Sirius system, who picks up a smaller Saturnian—still gigantic by human standards—en route to Earth.

birth to ripples there as a stone thrown into a pond produces concentric circles, and these undulations, repeated with a frequency of 400 billions, or even 1000 billions, per second, spread out to impact upon us and to disturb the movement of other stars that form the framework of our bodies. If these impacts increase their velocity of translation or rotation, we feel a sensation of heat; if, on the other hand, the constellations of our bodies were animated with more rapid movements, these shocks would make us lose speed, and we would experience a sensation of cold.

"When these intermolecular movements are produced in circumstances of a particular mass and velocity, they affect the eye; the undulations of these subtle little atmospheres strike the retina and cause the worlds that constitute it to vibrate in their turn. We see; we feel a luminous impression. I shall, moreover, come back to this point later in the discussion. I am not sorry to have shown that geologists, or rather mineralogists, are astronomers, veritable astronomers; they are occupied in *molecular astronomy*, instead of extending their explorations into the infinite spaces appropriate to the span of human sight.

"The only difference in is the order of grandeur. If there are animals on Earth that are infinitely tiny and intelligent, there might be veritable astronomers among them whose discoveries would bring the same enlightenment as ours to the celestial mechanics of those little Lilliputian worlds.

"I will further add, without fear of contradiction by astronomers, or even more so by mineralogists, that astronomy is, although it may not appear to be, dependent on mineralogy—and on the day when we shall have discovered the laws regulating molecular groups, the laws that govern the movements of the infinitely small, the astronomers will have no longer have anything to do but follow us."

Mr. Newbold: "You have just shown, gentlemen...."

("Louder!")

"....that the smallest particles of bodies are nothing but the reduced image of those great celestial bodies that whirl in the skies; but the Earth itself is nothing but a particle—a molecule, even—in the mass that we designate with the name *Milky Way*. We have there, writ very large, and very easy to study in consequence, a type of molecule that informs us of the physically-exact appearance of the least of the infinitely small molecules whose aggregation forms all the bodies that we see. We have only to pass from the great to the small to know what is happening in the infinitesimal molecular interstices that escape our most powerful instruments.

"What is the Earth? A sphere with a radius of 1,500 leagues,[22] whose constituent parts are continually augmented in density from the surface to the center. Since its origin, its materials have taken their places according to their density, the heaviest ones at the center, the lighter ones at the circumference. The floor on which we walk, the ground—a veritable rind, rigid and elastic—is no more than a thin pellicule, less heavy than that which precedes it. It is a raft continually floating on the internal matter; one can get an idea of its thickness by comparing it to the skin of a peach.

---

[22] A metric league is four kilometres, so this figure translates as a radius of 6,000 km. Modern measurements of the equatorial radius (the Earth is not quite spherical) give a figure of 6,378 km.

"At the center, the matter has more mass; its movements are more rapid; the temperature is higher. The higher one climbs, the less dense the matter becomes and its movements diminish in rapidity, communicating more easily with the loose matter distributed in space, and the temperature is much less. It even becomes low enough at a certain point for the material molecules to draw closer to one another and be juxtaposed tightly enough to form rigid ground; that is the Earth's crust.

"Beyond that, the temperature is variable, directly submissive to the influence of the Sun! Matter is more rarefied, bodies are gaseous; the aerial atmosphere succeeds the terrestrial crust and again one finds, as in the interior, a similar scale of density, much more matter being close to the surface than in the elevated layers. The aerial fluid also becomes more and more rarefied, confounded at its limit with the extremely tenuous matter that fills interplanetary space."

("We can't hear!")

"The following figures will give some idea of the successive decrease of the mass of matter from the center to the periphery:

Terrestrial globe	Atmosphere
10, 8, 6, 4, 2, 1	*1/2,000, 1/4,000, 1/6,000, 1/8,000*

"There is, as these proportions show, an abrupt transition at the surface. The disparate matter that is not included the scheme and which, in consequence, has less mass, overlies it.

"There is an excess of matter forced back to the surface by internal reactions: a sort of backwash. Little by little, this excess of matter finds its place in the interior, it settles back slowly, is organized and disappears.[23]

"The atmospheres of all the planets, in the immensity of time, are successively reduced in this manner; they condense by degrees, entering into stable combination. It should not astonish us, therefore, to see the heights of atmospheres diminishing progressively and their limits becoming more and more confused with the subtle and impalpable matter of the interplanetary medium.

"What I have just said, gentlemen, about our noble globe in particular—the terrestrial molecule—applies equally to all stars, all planetary molecules and all the constituent molecules of bodies. We shall find the same details, the same characteristics and the same laws in the myriads of particles that make up this table on which I am leaning, this hand, that inkwell, and all the objects that surround me.

"Lift up, by means of Archimedes' lever, any one of these little miniature worlds—the molecule that forms this grain of sugar, for example—and see it with 100 million times stronger than yours. That molecule, you

---

[23] This runs directly contrary to modern theory, which holds that planetary atmospheres gradually dissipate into space rather than being absorbed by solid surfaces; the difference has important consequences for the theory of planetary evolution that Parville subsequently puts forward, and hence for the theories of geological and biological evolution associated with it. Mr. Newbold's insistence on the central relevance of mineralogy to cosmology is understandable given Parville's education in the Ecole des Mines; his is, essentially, a geologist's view of the nature of the universe—but it is the view of a mineralogist rather than that of an evolutionary geologist of Charles Lyell's stripe.

have been told, is an assemblage of exceedingly tiny worlds—of atoms, if you wish to give them a name. But notice how beautiful it is. Here is our entire planetary system. There is the principal world, the Sun, then the secondary planets turning around it with vertiginous speed. Grasp the details and suppose that, with a pair of tweezers—incontestably gigantic relative to this sublime tenuousness—you were to seize one of these little worlds.

"It would be catastrophic, if you were able to do it, for to seize a world would be to destroy the equilibrium necessary to the existence of the ensemble. You would take away the movement with which it is endowed; you would annihilate it. Let us suppose it nevertheless.

"Well, you will find that it has an atmosphere and a solid crust, or, at the very least, matter that is more condensed, and, if you go towards the center, you will see the successive layers of that imperceptible atom disposed once again in order of density. Thus, a nucleus of condensed matter and an atmosphere of decreasing density make up the molecular world, the atom.

"Put these little worlds together and you will see them rotating with their atmospheres; you will have the molecules. Bring all the molecules together, and you will have the particle; you will have matter, with its form, as the eye perceives it.

"I have insisted, for my part, gentlemen, on this capital point, because, as you will understand, mineralogy and astronomy are not alone in sharing the privilege of this study. Geology provides the key to the intimate and primordial composition of matter. By means of deductions that are integral to it, it is permissible to go as far as the formation of the elements of bodies, and from there to ascend as far as the phenomena of chemical affinity, cohesion and elasticity.

"That is what I shall try to do, and to prove, on a more propitious occasion. It is necessary that the discussion does not stray too far."[24]

---

[24] Parville: "The theories expressed by these American gentlemen have the same initial effect as the fantastic elucubrations that emerge from diseased brains. In this regard, however, we are obliged to say that, in spite of their strangeness, they are completely in accord with the present state of positive science. Mathematical physics confirms these hypothetical facts, and Cauchy, our great geometer, says in his lectures at the College de France:

"Monsieur Ampère has deduced from observations the number of atoms that ought to enter into the composition of each integral molecule, with reference to the five forms of molecules admitted by mineralogists: tetrahedron, octahedron, primary parallelepiped, hexahedron and rhomboidal dodecahedron. He has found that the molecules comprising these five forms must be respectively composed of 4, 6, 8, 12 and 14 atoms. If, therefore, we were able to perceive the molecules of different bodies subject to our experience, they would present themselves to our eyes as species of constellations, and, in passing from the infinitely large to the infinitely small, we would find in the smallest particles of matter, as in the immensity of the skies, centers of action distributed relative to one another."

"Is that not what Messrs. Sieman and Newbold said, in their own terms?

"A well-known French scientist, M. A. Gaudin, a mathematician in the Bureau des Longitudes, has measured the distances separating these little stars, and their number, by a very ingenious method. It emerges from his researches that the distance between the largest organic molecules is a millionth of a millimetre, and he distance between the atoms is a ten-millionth of a millimetre. If one wanted to count the atoms

Mr. Siemen: "I thank our honorable president for the very interesting details that he has seen fit to provide to confirm my thesis. I hope that it might clarify more than one scientific matter that is still obscure."

Mr. Stek: "Will Mr. President be good enough to tell me whether, in his opinion, there are also mountains and upheavals on these little molecular worlds—whether the geological revolutions that have upset our world similarly afflict and modify their surfaces?"

Mr. Newbold: "That will not embarrass anyone, Mr. Stek. The causes that hold good on Earth also apply to the world of the infinitely small. The interior reactions proportionate to the size of these atomic planets must produce similar modifications, altering the surface—or, at the very least, the most resistant part of it, which must

---

enclosed in a little cube of matter two millimetres in each dimension, about the size of the head of a pin, and supposing that one could count *a million per second*, it would still take about 250,000 years."

The French mathematician Augustin-Louis Cauchy (1789-1857) had been dead for some years by the time this note was written, so the lectures in question and the cited observations of André-Marie Ampère (1775-1836) were considerably out of date by 1865. Ampère, early in his career, had attempted to produce a model to explain the six basic forms of crystals identified by René Just Haüy (1745-1822)—the list Parville gives omits a second variety of dodecahedron—but he was working with inadequate theoretical instruments and his model was eventually discarded and forgotten. The mathematician, chemist and inventor Marc-Antoine Gaudin (1804-1880), who nowadays most famous as a pioneer of photography, subsequently published a book developing the ideas mentioned here, *L'architecture du monde des atomes* (Gauthier-Villars, 1873).

be curved and lifted upwards in consequence of the forces in play. There are mountains and valleys, of that you may be sure—and what's more, that their direction and accidents are obedient to fixed and immutable laws. Must I remind you that on Earth, as I believe has been proven by someone that no one knows better than me, that there was not a single mountain chain whose direction was determined by chance? All mountains are directed according to firmly fixed axes.[25] Better still, one of my friends whom I regret not seeing among us, chief-engineer Mr. Nuevopolis,[26] has deduced admirably symmetrical facts from that. There is no longer any petty accident of the Earth's surface, be it a mountain pass, a river's mouth, a gorge, a spring or a mine, whose exact position cannot be determined mathematically. The anfractuosities of the ground, the depressions—everything is formed according to a deterministic law. That butte that hides the horizon from you, that hill, that valley, were they planted there by blind hazard?

"No, a thousand times no. All is harmony. Disorder is only apparent. Mr. Nuevopolis has brought that singular law, among other facts, into sharp relief, by discovering that every important accident, whether it be a spring, a node or a volcano, is always found at four-tenths of the total length of the envisaged group. If it is a river, describe a straight line between the mouth to the source. Mark the four-tenths; it is certain that that you will encounter there the most obvious accident in the

---

[25] Parville: "The same law has been recently established for the mountains of the Moon."

[26] Mr. Nuevopolis appears to be fictitious, and his "law" is certainly imaginary.

water's course. Similarly for a mountain chain, a seam of ore, etc.

"I can see no reason, Mr. Stek, why this curious symmetry should not also apply to molecules and molecular stars. All these undulations of the ground are merely the results of the vibration of matter; they obey the laws of musical harmony. And the phenomenon that causes a plate vibrating under the influence of a bow to remain in its place also causes certain parts of the ground to lift up and others to sink down, or not to quit their initial position.

"The laws of music are also those of geology. Everything is in everything. There is but one universal principle that animates matter, which gives it its different forms and its different properties."

("Good! Very good! We can hear!")

Mr. Greenwight: "Mr. President, the very important and very interesting considerations that our honorable colleagues and you have explained so well lead directly to astronomical applications of great philosophical significance. If the commission finds that the geological debate is exhausted, and if the geologists will authorize us to regard the rock discovered by Mr. Paxton has authentically extraterrestrial in origin, I ask for the floor to enter directly upon my subject and reveal the phases through which the celestial planets must necessarily pass, in order to address the question of the point in our sky from which this voluminous stone meteorite fell, whose presence here might modify existing ideas regarding the course and the equilibrium of heavenly bodies in the medium of space."

The large clock of Paxton House then sounded its seven sonorous chimes. The Sun had disappeared beyond the horizon. "Tomorrow! Tomorrow!" was the cry from several benches.

"Tomorrow, gentlemen!" roared the honorable astronomer, in sympathy. "The session has certainly been long, and I, more than anyone, will be happy to put an end to it."

Mr. Newbold: "The floor is accorded to Mr. Greenwight, and the session is ended."

(Ripples of laughter.)

It is a privilege granted to the great geologist to nominate the speaker and, when he feels disposed to yawn, to end the session. He thus gives satisfaction to the postulant and himself.

Enough for now. I fear that I might miss the boat to Fort Mann and the courier.

LETTER V

*The floor is Mr. Greenwight's. Matter and motion. How
are worlds made? The life of the stars. Transformation
of stars. How certain astronomers can still witness the
birth of our solar system in the present day. Why is the
Earth not brunette, Venus blonde, Mercury red-headed
and Mars albino?*

The discussion is going much more quickly than my
correspondence. By way of compensation and in order
not to abuse your hospitality I shall, to some extent, follow the example of reporters for daily newspapers with
regard to legislative debates. I shall resume the discussion, while allowing it to retain its own character, in the
fashion that debates inserted *in extenso* in the *Moniteur*
are continued; I shall similarly leap directly to the next
session in order to gain ground.

The floor has been give to Mr. Greenwight.

Mr. Greenwight: "Until now, gentlemen, we have
been talking about the infinitely small in nature; in my
turn, I want to say something about the infinitely large.
Mr. Sieman and Mr. Newbold, our honorable president,
have perfectly summarized our knowledge and our theories regarding the constitution of matter; I hope that I
might be permitted to draw consequences therefrom regarding the constitution of the universe, which I believe
to be important, and then, with the agreement of the
naturalists present, consequences regarding life on the
planets.

"Matter, primitively attenuated and in the state of
independent atoms, once filled space, inert and immobile. The Creator imparted movement to it, communi-

cating to it a certain quantity of force, forever imperishable. That initial force and the matter was the point of departure of all the transformations that have ever been, are, and ever will be.[27]

"All the physical forces that we see acting in the universe are only different manifestations of combinations of matter and the quantity of motions that it possesses. In the beginning, the independent atoms were obedient to the resultant of the forces that solicit them. They grouped themselves in regions and about centers, turning around one another according to the laws of mechanics. Thus was formed in places what we call *cosmic matter*, the veritable egg or embryo of a world.

"Condensed matter aggregated and continued its route through space, but, as time went by, an elastic reaction took effect; the quantity of motion of each cosmic

---

[27] Parville: "There would be nothing inadmissible, however, in supposing equally well that matter has been in motion eternally, that creation has neither an end nor a beginning. Why be astonished at that idea—is it not familiar to us? Is it that finite beings like ourselves can only conceive of the finite? The infinite escapes us by virtue of our very constitution." The statement in the text is strongly reminiscent of the opening passage of Lucretius' classic summary of Epicurean philosophy, *De rerum natura*, which was a very popular text in 19th century France. The poem argues that everything existent is "matter in motion;" it then imagines that there was a time when matter was evenly distributed in space and in uniform motion, but that *clinamen*—a tiny random swerve in the motion of one of the atoms—set off a chain of collisions that led to the current lumpy state of the universe: a sort of ultimate "butterfly effect." Mr. Greenwight, as a devout man, naturally substitutes God for *clinamen*, but leaves the subsequent hypothetical chain of cause-and-effect pretty much in place.

center diminished, being transmitted elsewhere and affecting new independent atoms. The force that was lost here was gained elsewhere; that is the ordinary state of affairs in this world—nothing is stable.

"At the point of origin, each group was animated by such a velocity that the constituent atoms rotated in extremely elongated trajectories. You know that motion and heat are synonymous; the latter is merely a manifestation of the former; it will not astonish you, therefore, that in that era, condensed matter was in a vaporous state. Eventually, however, as we have said, motion was necessarily lost, and so, in consequence, was heat. Matter cooled down; its constituent atoms circulated in tighter trajectories. Matter became liquid, and a world, disengaging from its first indecisive vapors finally showed itself in its spherical form. We say *a* world, but we should say worlds, for the condensed matter emerged, as it cooled, at several centers of action, and, in consequence, as many heavenly bodies, as many worlds.

"Note that the quantity of motion lost by that embryonic world—to follow but one among many—was rigorously and exactly gained by another center of action. That which had led to the liquid form here, and had contributed to the advancement of the world, determined another grouping of independent atoms elsewhere: an agglomeration of matter in a vaporous state, a new embryo destined to pass through different phases like the preceding one and eventually to transmit its force to another center of action. And so on, indefinitely!

"Time passes, and the embryonic world that we have picked out from all these condensations of matter at work loses more and more motion; the atoms agglomerate and form various combinations, all the while conserving their primitive directions. Molecules are born;

then, eventually, all those particular groupings that affect our sight and give us the various sensations corresponding to the various natural bodies. These are the little worlds that you have previously established so well. The heavenly body takes form; it gradually solidifies its surface in this fashion, and the screen thus formed greatly retards the loss of motion, and therefore the cooling of the matter.

"Thus you have seen it born; it lives; it has had its youth and its age of virility; it will have its old age; it will die. Let us follow it through this series of transformations.

"It will grow cooler incessantly; the physical conditions in which it finds itself will never cease to vary, from the most elevated temperature to the greatest cold we can imagine. Eventually, there will certainly come a time when it will have no further quantity of motion to lose; it will possess exactly as much of it as the subtle and tenuous matter composed of the independent atoms that fill space. Its temperature will be that of interplanetary space. It will have attained the final limit of life; a little further and it will be no more. It is, indeed, quite dead, but its matter nevertheless remains agglomerated and condensed for a long time—but not forever, for in that case all of space would gradually congeal and become solid, which would exclude the idea of the perpetuation of force.

"No, we must not forget that it is not alone in the group; it is only one stone in the edifice; the worlds that have the same origin, but which still possess life—motion—will yield and receive it in such a fashion as to disaggregate, so equilibrium is maintained. The quantity of motion is the same; the condensed matter has no more impulsion than the free and independent matter of space;

it recovers its liberty; the atoms disaggregate; the molecular groupings cease. The world vanishes; the construction collapses; only its materials subsist, to enter into new combinations elsewhere and to submit to new metamorphoses. From death, life is reborn. Everything is in everything.

"You see, gentlemen, that matter is drawn here, there and everywhere from the bosom of space, brought together by the initial force, then separated by the same force, taken elsewhere, recomposed again, and there is a perpetual labor of construction and destruction. One might say that there is not one grain of sand, not one molecule so infinitesimal that it is not obedient in every respect to that necessary and immutable law. Secondary forces make it and unmake it. In a word, matter and motion comprise nature entire."

("Hear hear!")

"Given these generalities, gentlemen, it is easy for me to embark upon my subject and determine—with some precision, I hope—the true relative ages of the planets. Let us go back to the creation of our system—and take note, gentlemen: although we have not been able to see that primitive epoch, others certainly have.

"Imagine yourselves, in fact, to be in a very distant solar system presenting at this moment the same physical characteristics as the Earth. Light travels, as you know, 298 million meters per second.[28] Now, for the inhabitants of that world, if it is distant enough, the formation of our world will have taken place millions of years ago, and yet they will only now be able to observe

---

[28] The text has "*lieues*" [leagues] instead of meters, which is presumably a misprint. Modern measurements give the slightly higher value of 299,792,458 meters per second.

it in that regions of the heavens. It is a simple matter of distance. It is necessary for the light that links the worlds in this sector of space to have time to reach its inhabitants. Thus, at this very moment, many astronomers lost in the oasis of the heavens can only witness the birth of our system.

"What happened? As always, a vaporous cloud is advancing through space at an extremely high temperature: a balloon of superheated vapors. At length, cooling takes place; the vapors contract and condense at certain points, obedient to the resultant of the forces that hold the in equilibrium. Where before there was only an opaline globe of hot vapor, new little globes form, less hot and more condensed, partly solidified, in exactly the same way that water vapor spread through the air forms a multitude of droplets as it cools.

"The initial cosmic matter is resolved into a rain of red hot drops: a rain of stars of worlds. We see them all around us; they fill the surrounding space again.

"Our Sun is but one scarcely-condensed drop of that fiery primitive matter; the planets are little droplets that sprang forth at the same time or condensed close to it. The initial motion that impelled the ensemble is conserved by each of its component parts, and all the worlds thus formed have continued to advance through space as before, rotating in the trajectories that the atoms were following before their agglomeration.

"Thus, in my view, it is established that the Sun and the planets have absolutely the same origin. In the beginning, at the moment when the cosmic rain condensed, they had the same constituents of uniform matter and the same quantity of motion—that which animated the entire system. The similarity was complete.

"Let us now follow these heavenly bodies through their transformations, through their evolution.

"Is it not perfectly clear that the quantity of movement that each one of them possesses cannot remain the same? If one considers it after a certain period of time, one will find it different. Is it not determined by the sum of free and independent primitive atoms, multiplied by the velocity with which these rudimentary heavenly bodies describe their trajectories?

"Now, we know that each petty atom inevitably loses its velocity over time, but that it loses it harmonically—which is to say that the loss is redistributed to every other atom. The more of them there are, the slower the loss of velocity is; the fewer there are, the more rapid it is. In other words, the loss of quantity of motion, which is the cooling of a heavenly body, is proportional to the sum of the atoms that constitute it—proportional to its mass. It is worth noting that this is no more than a translation of a principle well known to ordinary people: that the smaller a body is, the more rapidly it cools. From the preceding argument, gentlemen, you will immediately see this important consequence emerge.

"The rapidity of the evolution of a heavenly body, the duration of its life, is linked to its mass. Its life will be longer or shorter in proportion to the greater of lesser magnitude of its mass. From that emerges a method permitting the measurement of the age of a planet, and of forming an idea of the biological phenomena of which it has been the theater.

"Is not that which emerges from this reasoning process what common sense indicated in the first place? Why should you assume, gentlemen, a different plan of construction for every heavenly body? Why should not the Earth be hardened from the same clay as any other planet? Why should Venus be blonde and Jupiter brunette, Saturn chestnut, Mercury red and Mars albino? Why not the same constitution everywhere? What is here is there, what is there is here; once more, matter everywhere passes through the same evolutions. The only physical difference that the heavenly bodies present is in their age, the period of their transformation—that is all…"

The President: "Mr. Greenwight has just given a very clear summary of my idea—and that, I think, of all philosophical geologists—of the genesis of worlds. I…"

Mr. Greenwight: "I have not finished, Mr. President; the subject is large, and unless you have personal objections to address to me, I still implore the benevolent attention of the assembly."

Mr. Haughton, the geologist of the thorns and roses: "I request the floor."

Mr. Newbold: "I merely wanted to ask Mr. Greenwight to continue his account of geological evolution on another occasion. The floor, on that occasion, will be given to Mr. Haughton—but the advanced hour obliges me to ask my savant colleague to leave the conclusion of his interesting dissertation until tomorrow."

The session ended at 7 p.m.

LETTER VI

On the age of heavenly bodies. A means of determining it. By which it is shown that not all worlds can be inhabited. Objections. Elements of our solar system. Relationships that seem to exist between the volumes, masses and densities of planets. Different aspects. The necessary conditions for two worlds to resemble one another. The floor continues to be held by Mr. Greenwight.

Mr. Greenwight: "I showed in the last session that if worlds present different appearances, we must seek the cause solely in the greater or lesser rapidity of their evolution. In the epoch in which we see them, they are more or less advanced; they are younger or older, according to their initial mass.

"We might envisage them as different members of the same family. Each of them, save for a few characteristic and similarly-originated particularities, will at some time present the same form and the same appearance—but when they are all seen together, one is young and another old. It is the same with worlds. They are alive; they have all passed, or will pass, through the same phases, like every natural individual. It now remains for me to apply these considerations and to draw conclusions therefrom.

"I therefore propose to you a simple introductory stroll through our neighbor worlds; I hope to be able to specify their biological characteristics, their conditions of habitability.

"Firstly, before setting out, are they all habitable?

"Evidently not, gentlemen. The French scientist Arago,[29] and so many others who followed him, who placed inhabitants everywhere, even in the Sun, had no notion of the true laws that preside over the destiny of worlds.

"By an inhabitant—for it is necessary to define everything in order to avoid misconceptions—I mean some sort of animal, a living organism. Now, an organism can evidently only exist in a condition of being partially composed of liquids and solids. Liquids are generally the vehicles of life. For us, blood and the humors are absolutely necessary to the sustenance and the refinement of our organs. One cannot imagine any kind of creature solely formed out of solid materials; it would be inert. Such a body would belong to inorganic nature, here and everywhere else.

"That said, we arrive inevitably at this consequence: that no living being can exist on any world while the quantity of motion possessed by that world—which is to say, its own heat—is sufficiently elevated to vaporize the organism's liquids. Conversely, every organic creature will disappear from its surface when its heat be-

---

[29] Dominique-François Arago (1786-1853) was one of the most famous French scientists of his era, partly because he turned statesman after the revolution of 1848 and served as a government minister; his two brothers and his son also became famous as writers and politicians, though not as scientists. The notion that all heavenly bodies were inhabited, including the Sun, was a hangover from theological disputes regarding the plurality of worlds—which are discussed in more detail in the afterword—and crops up in numerous 19th century cosmological visions, including some by men of considerable scientific reputation, such as Humphry Davy.

comes low enough to freeze the organism's liquids. Those are the two extreme limits of life."

Mr. Rink: "But how can Mr. Greenwight tell whether the liquids of some heavenly body or other might not be able to resist high temperatures—and how, in consequence, the biological limits determining the appearance and disappearance of living beings can be determined?"

Mr. Greenwight: "Mr. Rink is a trifle hasty; everything cannot be said at once. It is evident that, at first glance, one cannot see why liquids might not have different properties of cohesion in the heavenly bodies of a system.

"A liquid's boiling point is linked to the pressure that it supports and its composition. If the pressure and the composition were significantly different, liquids might exist on each world at widely different temperatures, as Mr. Rink quite rightly says—but I have good reasons to believe that it is not so, and am drawn to the opposite conclusion.

"Yes, without a doubt, on Earth and elsewhere, pressure has varied since the time of origin; it must be more considerable at the beginning, and, in consequence, liquids could only evaporate at a higher temperature than they do now. Yes, I also think that the pressure might perhaps be slightly variable between stars, but within very narrow limits. In conclusion, though, considering the pressure that now exists on Earth and the neighboring worlds, recalling the unity of origin of heavenly bodies, and judging the past by the present, one is bound to admit that the composition of liquids of the same nature is much the same everywhere. We shall, moreover, return to this point soon and enter into some new explanations. Since composition and pressure remain almost identical, it can be presumed that the limits of existence are almost the same everywhere.

"At what temperature are the liquids of terrestrial organisms volatilized? About 80 degrees.[30] The pressure being much greater in the beginning, we shall extrapolate that initial temperature to 100 degrees. By the same token, we shall extrapolate to 30 degrees below zero the ultimate temperature—that at which freezing occurs in spite of the heat produced by vital activity. From 100 degrees to minus 30 degrees is 130 degrees; those are the degrees of life, the normal limitations circumscribing the existence of organisms.

"Thus, gentlemen, any world that possesses a surface temperature of 100 degrees cannot be inhabited. Any world that has cooled to below minus 30 degrees is similarly incapable of sustaining life. Conclusion: not all worlds are habitable.

"Let us see now which of those around us might be inhabited; let us seek to determine the age of each planet.

"The quantity of motion for each world, as we have already said, depends primarily on its mass. The different planets that surround us were doubtless absolutely

----

[30] It is not obvious why Mr. Greenwight selects this figure. He is obviously talking in degrees Centigrade (or Celsius), where the boiling-point of water is defined as 100 degrees, and the dissolution of any substance in water elevates its boiling-point. On the other hand, the rate of evaporation increases with temperature, and very few organisms—none of which Mr. Greenwight could have been aware—can long endure a temperature as high as eighty degrees. Mr. Greenwight evidently cannot imagine substances that are liquid over very different temperature-rages—methane, for example, or sulfur—forming suspension-media for life, but that is hardly surprising.

similar for a fairly considerable lapse of time,[31] during the entire period when they were still in a vaporous state, but they soon began to cool unequally, and since then, the conditions of existence and vitality have changed in each of them. Some have moved forward, others have remained far behind. Let us examine the matter.

"In order not to abuse the patience of the commission, I shall only take the worlds that surround us, those for which verification is to some degree possible—to wit, the Sun, Jupiter, Saturn, Neptune, Uranus, the Earth, Venus, Mercury and Mars.

"Here are the approximate masses of these worlds, as deduced by means of Newtonian attraction, in given in proportion to the mass of the Earth:[32]

The Sun	*354,930.000*
Jupiter	*338.034*
Saturn	*101.411*
Neptune	*20.879*
Uranus	*14.789*
The Earth	*1.000*
Venus	*0.885*
Mercury	*0.175*
Mars	*0.132*

---

[31] This is an arbitrary assumption that was subsequently opened up to very considerable doubt and is now considered to be—equally indubitably—quite false; unfortunately, Mr. Greenwight's entire theory of planetary evolution hinges on this poor assumption.

[32] Current estimates, made by the same method, only differ slightly, except with respect to Mercury, which Mr. Greenwight presumes to be a much more massive world than it is. Modern figures are: The Sun 332,946; Mercury 0.055; Venus 0.815; Mars 0.107; Jupiter 317.89; Saturn 95.17; Uranus 14.6; Neptune 17.2.

"Here now are the volumes of these worlds, their density and the intensity of the solar light and heat at the surface of each; elements of which we shall have need:[33]

Volumes in cubic myriameters:

Sun	1,520,976,847,653,880
Jupiter	1,528,718,930,570
Saturn	793,742,722,600
Neptune	113,604,675,800
Uranus	88,600,521,920
Eart	1,080,863,240
Venus	1,034,348,528
Mars	151,320,850
Mercury	64,851,800

Density:

Sun	1.4	Jupiter	1.3
Saturn	0.7	Neptune	1.8
Uranus	0.9	Earth	5.5
Venus	5.1	Mars	5.4
Mercury	6.8		

Intensity of solar light and heat relative to that of the Earth:

Jupiter	0.04	Saturn	0.01
Neptune	0.001	Uranus	0.003
Earth	1	Venus	1.9
Mars	0.4	Mercury	6.9

---

[33] In this table, it is the estimates relating to the two outermost planets that are the least accurate. Modern estimates of the volumes, relative to that of the Earth, are: The Sun 1,303,600; Mercury 0.056, Venus 0.86; Mars 0.15; Jupiter 1319; Saturn 744; Uranus 67; Neptune 57. If the figures in Mr. Greenwight's volume table were given on the same comparative basis as mine, they would be: The Sun 1,407,008; Mercury 0.060; Venus 0.96; Mars 0.14; Jupiter 1414; Saturn 734; Uranus 82; Neptune 105.

"If we consider the first of these tables,[34] it is evident that we shall find therein the order in which the worlds can be arranged according to the sum of their quantity of motion; we shall have their quantity of life, or, in other words, the duration of their existence.

"It is thus easy to see that the Sun is still only at the beginning of its evolution; it is in its infancy. Jupiter comes next, then Saturn, etc. The duration of the existence of these worlds is approximately expressed, taking the earth as unity, by the following figures: Sun 335,000; Jupiter 339; Neptune 20; Uranus 14; Venus 1; Mars 0.13; Mercury 0.17—which signifies that if the Earth were only capable of existing for a century, the Sun would last for 335,000 centuries, Jupiter 339 centuries, Neptune 20, Uranus 14, Venus only one, etc.

---

[34] The text says that the densities shown are relative to that of the Earth, although they are obviously given by comparison with the density of water, but makes no such qualification with respect to the subsequent table giving the intensities of solar radiation, which obviously are, so I have amended the indications accordingly. Modern estimates of planetary densities relative to that of water are: The Sun 1.409, Mercury 5.5, Venus 5.25, Earth 5.52, Mars 3.94, Jupiter 1.33, Saturn 0.71, Uranus 1.27; Neptune 1.77. The intensity of solar radiation is no longer considered an important datum, usually being replaced in modern tables with the surface temperature of each planet, which is dependent on the composition of its atmosphere and rate of rotation as well as its distance from the Sun, on the inverse square of which Mr. Greenwight's figures depend; because measurements of planetary distances were reasonably accurate at the time, so are his figures for the intensity of solar radiation.

"It is, however, necessary not to lose sight of the fact that this is only a matter of individual existence, for the various worlds that are individually dead will still remain aggregated until the complete separation of the group to which we belong, exactly as dead terrestrial matter still subsists for a long time before eventually turning to dust.

"The second table shows that the volumes occupied in space by these different worlds decreases with their mass, but not proportionately. Thus, Mars is less dense that Mercury even though its volume is greater.

"None of this should surprise anyone. We see similar phenomena on Earth and among small things. A body can diminish in mass and increase in volume, and *vice versa*. You know, for example, that as water freezes it increases in volume; ice is less dense than water. Bismuth is similar. Everything, in fact, depends on grouping: the arrangement of the constituent molecules. Now, you can explain these differences by going back to the genesis of the worlds. All of them were in a vaporous state. Each of them lost motion, and therefore heat, and, according to the rapidity of that loss, the atoms became grouped in one manner or another. The simplest combinations correspond to the most rapid cooling and, on the other hand, the variety of combinations must increase with the slowness of the evolution of the world.

"It is similarly impossible, gentlemen, not to recognize that the duration of each world's rotation on its axis must have had an influence on the greater or lesser condensation of its molecules. The centrifugal force dependant on the speed of rotation tends to disperse matter and increase the volume of the world; the proximity of the central nebulosity and its consequent attractive action must also have modified the phenomena of grouping, of atomic combination. There must therefore be a certain dependency between the density of each world, the duration of its rotation and its surface gravity. The speed of rotation disperses atoms, but the central attraction brings them closer together.

"Going back to the third table, which lists the densities of the planets, and setting them in relation to the duration of rotation and gravitation, one has:[35]

	Density	Duration of Rotation	Gravitation
Mercury	6.8	24h5m	5.63
Earth	5.5	23h56m	4.90
Mars	5.4	24h39m	2.1
Venus	5.1	23h23m	4.65
Neptune	1.8		5.00
Jupiter	1.3	9h55m	12.49
Uranus	0.9		5.44
Saturn	0.7	10h18m	5.34

"These seemingly-unrelated numbers are, on the contrary, a faithful translation of a general law of mechanics.

"It is, in fact, necessary to observe that not only does the speed of rotation play a large part in the dispo-

---

[35] Mr. Greenwight's estimated figures for the rotational period of each world were based on relatively primitive telescopic observations; the figures for Mercury and Venus are wildly inaccurate. Modern estimates are: Mercury, 58.7 days; Venus 243 days; Mars 24 hours 27 minutes; Jupiter 9 hours 55 minutes; Saturn 10 hours 14 minutes; Uranus 17.2 hours. Modern estimates of surface gravitation, relative to Earth, are: Mercury 0.38; Venus 0.90; Mars 0.35; Jupiter 2.64; Saturn 1.16; Uranus 1.17; Neptune 1.2. If Mr. Greenwight's figures were given on the same comparative basis they would be Mercury 1.15; Venus 0.95; Mars 0.44; Jupiter 2.55; Saturn 1.09; Uranus 1.11.

sition of atoms, but also the volume or radius of a world. The centrifugal force depends directly on its radius. By taking account of these various elements, not forgetting that the intensity of solar heat given in the third column as also played its part in modifying the grouping of molecules at the surface, we can arrive at the cause of the apparent anomalies that seem to exist in the densities of planets.

"A world, it may be mentioned in passing, will be as rich and as highly-developed as the quantity of life it has and the time of transformation it has before it.

"Why, then, is Mercury denser and smaller than Mars? One sees immediately that Mars rotates a little more rapidly and that its surface gravitation is much less. For these two reasons, the molecules have a tendency to lesser aggregation, or greater volume. One similarly sees that, relatively, it is on the surface of Mercury that the greater force of molecular grouping must exist—and, indeed, it is that planet that has the greater density. Equally, and for the same reasons, we find that the force of aggregation diminishes for the Earth, Mars, Venus, Jupiter and Saturn.

"These remarks are not without value, if one recalls Mr. Rink's objections. What tells you, our noble colleague asks, in effect, that the liquids on each world do not have a very different force of cohesion, which might permit them to resist high temperatures? And, indeed, when one sees that the forces of aggregation are so manifestly different, Mr. Rink's question is perfectly justified. We should, therefore, go on to point out that the age of a world has a disproportionate influence on the force of aggregation; the two are linked. We should not compare the force of two planets of widely different ages; the comparison is only admissible for worlds that have manifestly arrived at the same point of their evolution.

"On thus examining the Earth and Venus, whose masses are very similar and which have in consequence almost the same quantity of life, we evidently find the same density, the same speed of rotation, the same volume, the same gravitation. Here we may affirm that liquids behave as on Earth.

"Taking, by contrast, Earth and Mars, whose masses are in the proportion 1:0.13, the quantity of life being very different, a direct comparison is no longer possible. The density of Mars ought, in the first place, be greater than that of Earth, since Mars is more condensed—but it is very nearly equal. The fact is explained by observing that the surface gravity is less than half of what it is on Earth; it is absolutely necessary to take account here of all the elements that might modify the problem.

"Tomorrow if the President will authorize me to do it, I shall pursue these considerations."

LETTER VII

A stroll in the Heavens. The plurality of worlds. What is the Sun? A balloon of superheated vapor. Inhabitants of the Sun—none. Discovery of mines 38 million leagues from Earth. Why can one not see in the dark? Mr. Ziegler's opinion. Hemeralopia. Is Mercury inhabited? A word about Venus. Interplanetary humans. Of those who have been or are no longer. Situation on Earth. The Moon. Has it an atmosphere? How Mr. Greenwight settles the question. The Selenites.

The vice-president retains the floor.

Mr. Greenwight: "If I am not in danger of abusing the assembly's time, I shall now subject the principal planets of our solar system to a rapid review."

("Go on! Go on!")

"I have previously established, gentlemen, that the grouping of atoms and molecules is not only linked to the loss of each world's quantity of motion, but also depends on other elements, such as variations of gravitation, centrifugal force, etc.

"The combinations and the aspect of matter vary in each planet according to the value of these elements; we shall soon see within what limits. Let us examine each world with some care, and let us begin with the pivot of the solar system, the Sun.

"When one casts an eye over the elements of the solar system, one is easily convinced that the Sun must be the youngest, the least advanced of all the worlds; its evolution has scarcely begun; it has lost hardly any quantity of motion. At the very most, it is in the second phase of its existence, still in its infancy. If it were permissible to compare its life with that of a human being, I would say that it was six or seven years old at the most. Its matter is scarcely condensed, but the atoms that were once at liberty have drawn sufficiently close together to group themselves, having already formed gases and vapors. It is probably in an entirely gaseous state. The nucleus is doubtless only in the state of dissociated matter. We have not yet reached the time when the mass will become liquid. It is a mere balloon, a sphere of superheated gas enclosing solid particles, at least in the superficial regions that have cooled down to the greatest extent.[36]

---

[36] Parville: "This opinion is entirely in conformity with that issued at the French Académie des Sciences by a highly-esteemed astronomer, Mr. Faye. After studying the appearance of sunspots on more than 5000 photographs taken by Mr. Carrington, Monsieur Faye has arrived at the conclusion that the Sun is not, as Wilson, Herschel and Arago would have it, a solid globe covered by a cloudy layer and then a "luminous atmosphere," nor, as Kirchhoff would have it, a liquid globe surrounded by a single atmosphere. It is still a gaseous sphere whose superficial parts tend to combine chemically. The associated parts become heavier and fall into the depths; they are replaced at the surface by new matter, which aggregates in its turn and falls back. That causes vertical currents. The rising matter dispatches from its trajectory the uniquely luminous superficial parts, and the inhabitant of Earth perceives a dark hollow surrounded by brilliant bands. Thus, one can explain the different appearances of the spots."

The individuals cited who have not previously annotated are Hervé Faye (1814-1902), Richard Christopher Carrington (1826-1875), Alexander Wilson (1714-1786), William Herschel (1738-1822) and Gustave Robert Kirchhoff (1824-1887).

"Research carried out in Europe by means of spectral analysis has demonstrated the existence within the Sun of several terrestrial metals reduced to vapor. This tends to prove—and I recommend this example to Mr. Rink—that the atoms adopt certain groupings everywhere, in spite of differences of mass, gravitation, etc.

"This demonstrates in addition, that the formation of certain composites occurs at enormous temperatures, and that chemists, unless they find a means of creating a similar temperature, have no chance of attaining the isolation of atoms in order to decompose reputedly simple bodies.

"Finally, it is permissible also to conclude from this that mines, the metal seams that traverse terrestrial rocks, are really no more than infiltrations of central matter still in ebullition. I do not insist on these consequences; they are more familiar to the savant chemists included in his assembly than they are to me.

"The Sun will continue its evolution as time passes. It will grow old and cool like other worlds, but it will certainly remain the last in the system, and when all the other centers of motion in our cooling system are dead, it will still be alive and will survive for a long time yet, alone in the immensity of space. It is not most certainly not inhabited at this moment. Can you imagine organisms living at the vaporization temperature of silver? Vaporous organisms?

"An organism—and this is perhaps a definition—requires an assemblage of solid, liquid and gaseous elements in a continual state of reaction; now, the Sun still possesses only one of these necessary elements; its organisms are in the process of elaboration, nothing more. Will they appear in future? Why not? Life seems to reside in a given quantity of motion, just like heat and light. Too great a quantity of motion and heat becomes light; not enough, and light becomes merely heat; too much quantity of motion, and you prevent matter from organizing itself or reflecting in itself that quantity of motion; too little, and the end to be attained is lost again. Exactly the right quantity is required. That is why you see life manifesting itself only at certain temperatures, and disappearing in the same way. Mr. Ziegler, who has explained his ideas in this regard to me, shares my opinion; he will address the subject much better than I can; I shall therefore pass on, and content myself with saying that I do not see why the Sun should not welcome inhabitants later on."

Mr. Newbold: "Does Mr. Greenwight think, the Sun being the conservator and regulator of force and not receiving light or heat from any neighboring star, that its inhabitants might live in the most profound darkness?"

Mr. Greenwight: "I am perhaps not competent to answer my honorable president, but I ask the physiologists, Mr. Rink, Mr. Wintow and Mr. Ziegler, whether it is not perfectly admissible that certain creatures, even of a superior order, can see in the dark?"

Mr. Wintow: "I agree entirely with Mr. Greenwight's opinion; we have animals on Earth that can only see at night; it's a matter of the adaptation of the retina. Most animals are conformed in such a fashion that solar light does not inconvenience them. It is rather like a trigger that requires activation; the trigger is tight here because the force is great, but is can be the case that a much less powerful force could activate it if it were slackened. The trigger is the optic nerve, the force is the quantity of motion. The quantity of motion, the caloric [37] inherent in the Sun itself, is doubtless sufficient to stimulate the retina, in order that the organisms of that star might see."

Mr. Ziegler: "in support of what my savant colleague has just said, I will add that, when solar light has acted too strongly, when the force has overstimulated the retina and modified the elasticity of the nerve, human beings can no longer see anything at all once the Sun has disappeared beyond the horizon; the sensitivity is blunted. This affliction, which physicians call hemeralopia, is most often encountered among soldiers, in sentries obliged to remain exposed to the Sun's ardor for long periods of time. They can be cured by restoring the nerve's elasticity; to do that, the invalid is kept in a dark room for several days. This example, combined with many others, leaves me in no doubt that. Organisms will be able to see quite well in physical conditions other than those present on our planet."

Mr. Greenwight: "I therefore conclude, gentlemen, that the Sun will, in all probability, be inhabited one day—but millions of years will pass yet before the quantity of motion the world possesses will decline to the point of permitting life to develop there.

"The first world encountered in space in going from the center to the periphery is Mercury. Following the order of masses, it is the eighth; it is one of the worlds whose evolution is furthest advanced. A long time has

---

[37] "Caloric" was the name given to an obsolete "principle of heat," a supposed form of matter to which the phenomena of warmth and combustion were once ascribed; Mr. Wintow is evidently attempting to redefine it in terms of motion rather than matter.

already passed since it was vaporous or liquid; its solidified surface must therefore have a rather considerable thickness. Its density is 6, the largest; its gravitation 5, stronger than the Earth's. The solar heat is represented by the figure 7, that of Earth being 1. If we continue to reckon in terms of a human life, Mercury must be about 35 years old.

"Matter condensed there more rapidly than elsewhere; its combinations must have been less numerous there than in the other worlds. As for organisms, it is quite certain that they exist and that they have already existed for a long time. They must differ from terrestrial organisms, but within restricted limits. Inversely to what we said about solar organisms a moment ago, it is necessary here to imagine a much more resistant retina to permit organisms to see in a luminous environment as intense as that of Mercury.

"The creatures must also be of an inferior order to those of Earth—smaller in size. Liquids must form at more elevated temperatures than those on Earth, because the pressure there is greater. Perhaps organisms were able to develop when the temperature reached 200 degrees; in any case, the higher creatures on the scale would only have been able to appear later. Mercury is advanced enough for us to be able to say that a species homologous with humankind must already have existed on the planet; it must now be inhabited by the homologues of the human species destined to replace us on the Earth.

"There is, in fact, no reason to refuse the supposition that all species are replaced in parallel on every world, in accordance with successive biological conditions; it follows that, on every advanced world, if it were possible to dig a shaft through the series of layers that compose it, one would discover the sequence of creatures that had existed on the surface, including species that presently have counterparts and analogues on more slowly-developing worlds. In the same way, a shaft on a slowly-developing world would reveal the past of the advanced world—a question of phases and continuous evolution. Let us pass on. [38]

Venus is undoubtedly the world most similar to the Earth in all its physical conditions. If a profound conviction could qualify as an argument in scientific matters, I would not hesitate to claim that a voyager suddenly transported from our world to Venus would not find himself any more disorientated than if he had been taken blindfold to some other region of the Earth: the same quantity of life, very nearly, emerging from the same matter, the same nature and the same inhabitants, perhaps a little more advanced than on Earth.

This is what theory says; observation confirms it in every point. One discovers mountains, an atmosphere identical to that of our world, with trade winds like those

---

[38] Parville: "Some people might object that the very different surface gravities of worlds might lead to very different constitutions. Thus, on the Sun, a man made like one of us would weigh 2000 kilograms instead of 70 kilograms. He would not, therefore, have enough muscular strength to get up again if he fell down. This objection is illusory, because life and muscular force depend on the force of aggregation of the given world, and that force of aggregation is proportional to the gravitational attraction itself. The proportionality holds true in its entirety; if the gravitation is greater, the muscular force increases in consequence." This is not a sound argument, in terms of contemporary science; muscular strength in not proportionate to density.

in our tropical regions.[39] The inhabitants must therefore be almost completely identical to us, and if one dug down into Venus one would probably find the same sequence of creatures there as on Earth. The organisms there have developed in parallel. Born and living in the same eras, Venus and Earth will die in the same era.

The Earth, like the preceding planet, is still in the early phases of its evolution. It is young, it is adolescent; perhaps it is no more than 20 or 21 years old. It is not long since the quantity of motion it possesses has become small enough to permit the existence of superior beings; the series of its creatures will doubtless take a long time yet to perfect itself—because, it is worth mentioning in passing, once a world has cooled sufficiently for the solidification of its surface to take place, the loss of caloric only takes place thereafter with extreme slowness. One can even add that, so far as we are concerned, the Earth has not lost any heat during historic times.

"Here, for the first time, we find a satellite: the Moon. The Earth is to the Moon what the Sun now is to the Earth. In the beginning, the Earth was the Moon's sun, and the Moon was a little planet lit by that secondary sun. Since then, the little planet has lived, and has gone through a fraction of the phases of its existence; when the Earth descended to the rank of planet, it descended itself to the rank of satellite.

---

[39] The mountains were illusory, and it is not clear how the supposedly identical composition of the atmosphere had supposedly been "discovered" rather than merely assumed. Spectroscopic analysis, when it eventually became feasible, revealed that the atmosphere of Venus is, in fact, very different in composition from Earth's.

"The Moon is old; its mass is 1/80 of the Earth's; it has therefore lived 80 times faster; it must be solidified in large part, and very cold. We shall make an observation here that is very important, and which probably provides the best indicator of he advanced age of a world: I mean the atmosphere.

"What is a world's atmosphere? Gentleman, I consider this fluid envelope as the residue, or the smoke, of the internal chemical reactions that have formed the world. At the moment of solidification, the lightest vapors escape through fissures and rise above the vapors susceptible of being condensed and producing primitive ground. An atmosphere must be constituted in the beginning by complex compounds which, as cooling progresses, are further aggregated and become solid or liquid.

"In consequence, a progressive process of triage is produced—a purification—and only the most elementary compounds remain above the crust: those present in too great an excess to enter into rapid combination, or whose weak density distanced them from the surface. These fluid compounds condense slightly every day, by reason of cooling, but so slowly that we cannot yet perceive it.

"In addition, they move undetectably from without to within by a process of endosmosis,[40] and slowly combine with the interior materials, to the extent that every atmosphere is destined to condense, diminishing by de-

---

[40] Parville has "*endomose*" and might conceivably mean something other than endosmosis. In either case, the synthesis of the term from the Greek adds nothing to the description he has just given; such restatement terms do not qualify as explanations.

grees until it eventually disappears entirely. Thus, every young world has a complex and dense atmosphere; every old world only preserves traces.

"There is nothing surprising, therefore, in encountering atmospheres on Venus and Earth that are fairly pure and not very dense. Nor is there anything surprising in finding no trace of one on the Moon; it must be so lacking in density and height that it can escape our observation. Nevertheless, a rough and approximate calculation can at least furnish us with some clarification on this point.

"We can assume, without straying too far from the truth, that, at the outset, the heights of the lunar and terrestrial atmosphere were proportional to the radius of each world and inversely proportional to their gravitation, density and mass. On submitting these givens to calculation, one finds that the height of the lunar atmosphere must now be about 80 times less than that of the terrestrial atmosphere.[41]

"Now, the height of the terrestrial atmosphere measures at least 30 leagues.[42] The lunar atmosphere must therefore still extend about 1500 meters. It is no

---

[41] Parville: "h = (0.1x1)/(80x1/6)x(5/3) = 30/2400 = 1/80" This arithmetic formulation is obviously mis-rendered; the calculation is wrong because, based on the verbal formulation, there is a term missing. It should be observed, however, that the terms listed are not independent of one another and that the equation is needlessly overcomplicated in consequence; its resultant, 1/80, is identical to one of the included terms (the ratio of masses), the others cancelling one another out. The whole operation is nonsensical in terms of modern theory.

[42] Parville: "It has been assumed until recently that the Earth's atmosphere did not extend beyond 18 leagues, but European astronomers are indeed tending to set the limit much higher."

wonder that we no longer perceive any trace of it. Its density must be so feeble, in fact, that it must correspond to that of the air which remains in our pneumatic machines when we have created a void therein.

"The atmosphere of the Moon bathes the bases of its high mountains [43] as the sea bathes our coasts. In a few more thousands of years, all the lunar gas will have been absorbed into the world's mass.

"The old age of the Moon is further attested by its density. The force of aggregation on our satellite is, for an equal quantity of motion, much less than that of the Earth, and yet its density is three-fifths of Earth's. This is the result of extreme cooling and a great depletion of the quantity of motion.

"Is the Moon inhabited? I think not. Has it been? I am convinced of it. Organisms must always have been subject to less pressure there than on Earth; they ought to have appeared later than on Earth at a similar degree of cooling; they ought, by the same token, to disappear later. Liquids, indeed, were only able to form there at a lower temperature than on Earth, and solids to constitute themselves at a similarly lower temperature. In sum, everything encourages the belief that, existence there being more rapid, the creatures must have been inferior, smaller and more delicate.

"We do not believe that any inhabitants still exist, for there are no longer any liquids [44] on the lunar sur-

---

[43] Parville: "The lunar mountains surpass 7000 meters.

[44] Parville: "There are no more liquids because they have all evaporated as a result of the tiny atmospheric pressure. They have undoubtedly been fixed in combination with solids; otherwise, one would still sometimes perceive them in the atmos-

face; if they do exist, they can only belong to the most infinitesimal ranks of organic creation, perhaps organisms buried deep in the ground, which have so far escaped freezing.

"The observation needs to be made here that, in addition to a world's own heat, it is necessary to take account of the radiant heat of its illuminating world. Now, it is quite certain that lunar cooling was once tempered by the neighborhood of the Earth, as it was then and is now by solar radiation; the preceding results therefore offer no more than a simple and crude approximation. This remark is worth making, for it seems to me that the development of life also depends greatly on the sum of motion transmitted by the principal world.

"I beg the assembly's pardon for developing my considerations at such length, but they bear directly on the subject. I am happy to explain my views and submit them to the criticism of the most illustrious scientists in the New World. This will perhaps be a unique opportunity for me, and I am taking advantage of it. Tomorrow, I shall examine the conditions of the habitability of Mars, the planet that seems the most interesting of all in the context of this debate.

---

phere in the form of clouds, of which one never sees any trace."

LETTER VIII

From world to world. Sequence. On the planet Mars. Seas, continents and ice-caps. Why men existed on Mars a long time ago. Inferior beings. The mummy. Jupiter is indeed Jupiter. Still liquid. Do not, therefore, place inhabitants everywhere. Why one would like to be a man on Jupiter. Their supremacy. Saturn. Neptune and Uranus. Life in the worlds. Summary. Real estate in the future.

Mr. Greenwight: "I shall be brief, gentlemen, and remind you of the fundamental characteristics of Mars: density 5.1; gravitation 1/2; rotation 24 hours; mass 1/8 that of the Earth.

"These figures establish that Mars is in advance of us, and that its cooling must be considerable. A long time has already passed since vital conditions analogous to those of Earth have disappeared from its surface. Its rotation is very similar to that of our globe, but is gravitation is much smaller; the forces of combination there are less, and its density would be inferior to that of the Earth if the more advanced cooling had not further condensed matter there, for which reason it is almost equal.

"The lesser surface gravitation implies that organisms must have appeared at a lower temperature than on Earth, and must also have disappeared at a lower one. They ought still to exist, though, and the creatures that live there now belong to a stage more highly advanced than Earth's present human beings. It is necessary to go back to a much earlier epoch to find an analogue of the human species. Do I need to say that the organisms of Mars must nevertheless be some way behind those of

Earth? Life there is more rapid, the creatures less susceptible of improvement.

"The mummy from the planet Mars, if that is where it originated, must therefore come very close to representing the human type of Mars analogous to the human type of Earth. On the evidence of the amphorae and other objects discovered by Mr. Paxton, we have the right to suppose that this type belongs to one of the planet's earlier human species. One can even conclude, tentatively, from the form of the vases that the human mind passes through the same phases and undergoes the same transformations everywhere—but I should not anticipate; that will enter into the discussions later. If my colleagues the chemists of the assembly will permit me, I should simply like to recommend to their attention the molecular grouping of the aerolith—the density of the matter. It follows from what I have said that the aerolith ought to differ in this respect from terrestrial bodies of the same nature, since the elements vary with the age of a world. The substance of which the mummy is made, the bones, ought not to have exactly the same density or the same chemical composition as similar terrestrial compounds.

"I shall add in conclusion, gentlemen, that the telescopic examination of Mars seems to have revealed continents, seas and ice-caps there—which provides full confirmation of my expectations.[45]

---

[45] Parville: "Mars is, after the Moon, the world best known to astronomers. The planet's disk presents dark and light stains of different colors. The contours are more luminous than the central part. Finally, at two opposite points—at the two poles—two bright patches are clearly discernible. All these features of the planet vary with the seasons. It is assumed that

"The atmosphere seems to be denser than ours. That is entirely consistent with the cooling and with the lesser power of aggregation possessed by the world; it would require more time to absorb its atmosphere. As I have observed to Mr. Rink, the physical aspect of Mars seems to prove that, in spite of the differences in the characteristic elements of each planet, matter there appears to take much the same forms; we find liquid, ice and solid materials on Mars entirely analogous to ours, if the aerolith really can provide us with a specimen of it.

"Finally, the juxtaposition of ice and liquid makes the important role that solar radiation plays in the conservation of life perfectly evident. Without the Sun,

---

the reddish and light areas of Mars are the solids parts—the continents—and that the darker bluish areas are liquid. As for the polar patches, they are evidently made of ice, for, when spring arrives in one hemisphere that path visibly diminishes while the one in the opposite hemisphere increases. The ice-cap in the southern hemisphere is larger than the one in the northern hemisphere, which is easily explained by the inclination of the planet's axis; the northern pole receives more heat than the southern pole, the quantities of heat received being in the ration of seven to five. If there is ice on Mars it is because there is snow, water, and rain, and in order for there to be water, it is necessary that there should also be an atmosphere to retain it in the liquid state. The meteorological conditions of the planet Mars must therefore resemble ours quite closely. These are, at least, the conclusions that have been drawn from the research of the German and English astronomers Beer, Mädler and John Phillips."

The references are to Wilhelm Beer (1797-1850), Johan Heinrich von Mädler (1794-1874) and John Phillips (1800-1874); Parville's text misrenders the second name as "Moedler" and the third as "Johns Philips."

Mars would undoubtedly be too cold to conserve matter in a liquid state on its surface.

"You see, gentlemen, that I am content to sketch out the physical characteristics of the world; I shall leave the work of extrapolating the physiological and biological aspects of the subject to the competent scientists. I shall rapidly conclude my voyage of exploration.

"Jupiter comes next after Mars. Fundamental characteristics: density, 1.3, very similar to that of the Sun, 1.4; rotation 9 hours; mass 342 times that of the Earth; gravitation 2.5.

"After the Sun, it is certainly Jupiter that conserves the greatest quantity of motion; it is very young, in its infancy, and its surface has scarcely begun to solidify. It density is also low, and its atmosphere must be extensive and dense. Bands are, in fact, visible on its disk, which leave no doubt regarding the considerable gaseous envelope that surrounds the world.

"Let no one tell us, thoughtlessly, that Jupiter possesses inhabitants. It is too much to imagine that any but the most primitive organisms might have developed there as yet. Later, the successive creatures of the scale of life will be found there, entirely in correspondence with the varying temperature of the world, but at the present point in its evolution Jupiter is not yet accessible to complex creatures. Organisms will, moreover, develop there gradually; everything tends to imply, given its greater quantity of motion, that they will be superior to those of Earth, and superior to those of all the other worlds in our solar system—but we shall certainly have been gone for a long time when the species analogous to the present-day Earthly human species makes its appearance on Jupiter. The flora and fauna there will certainly be more complex and more perfected than anywhere else. Mythology was right: Jupiter is indeed Jupiter.

"It has four satellites, four little planets warmed by this secondary sun. They must be inhabited now by inferior organisms.

"After Jupiter comes Saturn: mass, 103; rotation, 10 hours; density 0.7; gravitation 1.

"After Jupiter, this is the youngest planet; it must, however, be solidified at its surface. The great quantity of motion that it still possesses and its rotation—considerable in proportion to its diameter—explain its low density. In all probability, Saturn can only be inhabited by primitive organisms.

"This planet presents, as you know, a singular anomaly: it is surrounded by a large equatorial ring, which floats in space without touching it. In the beginning, matter was carried towards the equator of the world by centrifugal force; then, when cooling began, it must have been unequal, and the equatorial layer must have been separated, continuing on its path and following the rotation of the world as if it were still an integral part of its mass. The further the cooling progressed, the further away the ring drew; it even broke up into several secondary rings—which appears to me to be irrefutable proof of its solidification. Having little mass, in fact, it would soon have lost enough motion to solidify. The curious fact is that the ring is, in sum, a satellite, and that organisms must have developed, and doubtless still subsist, there. They must not be very far advanced on the scale of creatures, but if they have sufficient sentience to conceive the beauty of the spectacle that surrounds them, they must have fallen into ecstasy more than once before the magnificent globe that moves through the medium of space along with them, providing them with light and heat.

"The inverse will soon be manifest, and the future inhabitants of Saturn will enjoy the singular view of that immense ring, which separates them from the heavens like an immense guard-rail. Saturn has seven satellites, doubtless too cold to permit life to exist there still.

"Neptune, which comes next,[46] has a mass of 87, a very low density of 1.8 and a gravitation of 1.33. It receives very little of the Sun's warmth, and must already have cooled too far to permit the development of organisms. Because of its distance, its speed of rotation remains undetermined; given its low density, we think that it must be considerable.

"Uranus only has a mass of 77, older than Neptune and, in consequence, more distant still. It has a very low density, comparable to that of Saturn, 0.9; gravitation 2/3; rotation unknown but certainly very rapid. Matter there is not very condensed, in spite of the greater cooling relative to the preceding planets, but doubtless sufficient to give birth to organisms.

"I have finished, gentlemen, and will summarize this overly long excursion through the constituent molecules of the celestial corpus of which we are a part. I have briefly described the conditions of habitability of planets. I shall repeat them now in a few words, so that each of you might make a good guess as to the world from which the strange individual discovered by Messrs. Paxton and Davis might have come. Here, as elsewhere,

---

[46] In fact, Uranus comes next in the orbital sequence, and clearly did so in the earlier table showing the relative intensities of solar radiation; this seems to be a simple error born of carelessness.

theory will doubtless be able to guide us toward the truth.

LIFE IN THE WORLDS

Sun: uninhabited as yet.

Mercury: inhabited; primitive creatures; homologues of future terrestrial species.

Venus: inhabited; creatures entirely analogous to those of Earth; corresponding fauna and flora.

The Earth: inhabited for a long time already, and will be for a long time yet.

The Moon: no longer inhabited, but has been.

Mars: inhabited; creatures analogous to those of Earth, smaller and inferior; homologues of Earthly species a long time ago; now inhabited by creatures corresponding in the organic scale to the future inhabitants of Earth.

Jupiter: not yet inhabited; satellites inhabited.

Saturn: primitive creatures; satellites possibly still inhabited.

Neptune: doubtless inhabited by primitive creatures.

Uranus: rudimentary organisms.

"It is sufficient, gentlemen, to run through this summary to be convinced that the interplanetary man, if he really does have an extraterrestrial origin, can only have come, according to this list, from the planet Venus or the planet Mars.

"All the geologists will doubtless share my opinion when I say on my own behalf that I have no hesitation in choosing between the two hypotheses and opting for Mars.

"Venus and the Earth have matched one another step for step, or very nearly; now, humans cannot have existed on Earth when the aerolith fell, since the appearance of the human species on our globe is posterior to the deposit from which the bolide was recovered; therefore, the analogous type cannot have existed yet on Venus.

"On the other hand, it follows from the preceding argument that the Martian homologue of the terrestrial human species must have made its appearance in an epoch considerably anterior to ours; there is, therefore, nothing astonishing in encountering one in an ancient geological stratum. Finally, if—as it is permissible to suppose—the dimensions of organisms on each world are proportional to their volumes, the relative smallness of the mummy points to a Martian origin.

"One sees, therefore, when all is said and done, that theory accords very well with the sketch of our solar system inscribed on the plate found in the aerolith. When one sees that Mars, whose volume is smaller than that of the neighboring planets, is drawn larger, and sets that beside the distances separating the Sun, Mercury, Venus and the Earth, the first idea that springs to mind is surely that the sketch was made by a creature native to Mars.

"Given this, I therefore agree wholeheartedly with the conjectures of Messrs. Paxton and Davis. As considerations departing from a very distant point draw us by a different route to the same conclusion, I have no hesitation in drawing the attention of the assembly to the striking coincidence; it is a strong argument in favor of the hypothesis of the fall of a genuine inhabitant of the planet Mars.

"Such is, gentlemen, the thesis that I want to develop, and I thank you for having listened to me with such indulgence."

Mr. Stek: "Mr. President, I ask permission to make the observation to Mr. Greenwight that he has forgotten the Moon."

Mr. Greenwight: "The mummified individual that has been discovered here is explicable without taking a further step. I should like to say to my honorable opponent that, in all probability, the lunar homologue of the terrestrial human species would also be proportional to the volume of the satellite. Now, if one compares the volumes of the Earth, the Moon and Mars, one finds that the dimensions of a man of the Earth's surface and those of the interplanetary man are in the same ratio as the volumes of our world and Mars; when one makes the comparison with the Moon one finds a height much too considerable. The inhabitants of the Moon must certainly have been smaller than us, to a fairly considerable extent. It was for that reason, which is as good as any other, in parallel occurrence, that I neglected to take our satellite into account. Moreover, I shall ask here for the support of the chemists. The density of the aerolith might shed some light on the question."

Mr. Liesse: "Tomorrow we shall know the density of the principal specimens of the aerolith."

Several members came to congratulate Mr. Greenwight. The session ended at 5 p.m.

LETTER IX

The conference hall. News of the aerolith. Nothing new comes of it. The journalists' bench. Seringuier yawns. Williamson criticizes. What a singular little man Williamson is! A portrait on the hoof. Noirot de Sauw. A cross between a Chinese and an Austrian. Literary patchworks. Abbé Omnish. Might the interplanetary man have come from the Moon? What matter answers. Messrs. Haughton and Ziegler. Are you a materialist, sir? Spontaneous generation in America. What is life?

The conference hall is even fuller than on previous days. The discussions are making progress, it is true, but curiosity-seekers are arriving in ever-greater numbers. Several boats and convoys have to be employed to maintain provisions to Paxton House. The owner has had even more log cabins built. The proceedings are literally crowded out; the aerolith is surrounded and people are pressed against the windows of the hall, avid to catch snatches of the discussion. Many people, fortunately, come in the morning from Fort Ben and go back there in the evening.

The immense bolide has now been entirely perforated, but without any new results. Mr. Vanbrée, Mr. Davis and several more of the commission's geologists have explored the surroundings, to see if other specimens of interplanetary rock might be found—a few fragments analogous to our little present-day aeroliths—but the research is very difficult in a milieu of virgin forest, genuinely impenetrable without recourse to axes and fire.

We are almost all present on the journalists' bench. Abbé Omnish, Seringuier and Noirot de Sauw find the debates very tedious; Seringuier, however, bears his irritation patiently and writes articles for a popular almanack. "The public reads it," he says, "stupid or not—what does it matter? With my name at the bottom, and the Hacken imprint, if the book were stitched together from blank pages they'd still find it very interesting." He's right, though! The public is naïve.

Williamson, a very short man who would like to make as much noise as four, but who cannot contrive to do so with his confused prose, criticizes Greenwight, Newbold Stek, the debates and everything else. He would criticize himself if he dared! Williamson, under the pretext of writing about science, preaches every Sunday for two long columns in the *Strand*, a daily newspaper. Do you think, perhaps, that he is occupied in popularizing the question on the agenda? Bah! The matter is too simple for him; he writes as if the readers were familiar with it; he puts the cart before the ox by discussing, seriously and sententiously, the scientific method. He criticizes again and always, without noticing that he is crying in the wilderness! Criticism is very interesting, but it is necessary to know, before all else what is being criticized. What does it matter, readers of the *Strand*, provided that Williamson is criticizing? A veterinarian by profession, I believe, he dives into questions of astronomy and mechanics with an admirable bluntness; he never bothers with matters of veterinary art. He calls this treating science without prejudice, as if science were not SCIENCE! What a priceless little fellow!

Last year, lectures were much in vogue in Richmond. He advertised the opening of his course in all the newspapers and plastered the walls with posters. "No hall," he said, "will ever be great enough to contain my audience." Alas, poor colleague, the day arrived all too quickly. The professor had to share the same fate as your eccentric Ampère. You will recall that one day, when the weather was bad, having arrived at the College de France by cab, he began his lesson and concluded it in front of a single very attentive listener. Absorbed by his subject, he expended the time in the regular manner, then looked at his watch and said: "Oh, I beg your pardon, Monsieur, for having kept you for such a long time." The listener looked at him in astonishment. "But Monsieur knows perfectly well," he said, "that I have the time to spare; has he not hired me for an hour?" Alas, Ampère's sole listener was his cab-driver!

It was the same for Williamson, who—being less distracted, and with good cause—had plenty of time to be vexed by the circumstance. One sole disciple presented himself, and this single listener was the agent for his course. Williamson has abandoned lecturing. In addition, the Richmond Medical Academy has quite categorically refused him one of its vacant chairs. Williamson will have to grow much older before growing in stature.

Noirot de Sauw, as stunted as an old Norman apple tree tormented by the years, hides his ignorance in his confidence. He is well past sixty; he is bent over; in his profile he resembles a chimpanzee, without any flattery; in his face, he is a living Egyptian mummy. What a singular individual! In private life he bears a name with a particle, which gives way to a simple parenthesis at the end of his articles. Although his name is almost French, he does not resemble a Frenchman in appearance or character; he is more like a cross between a Chinese and an Austrian.

The style resembles the man: old, stunted, dry and taut, without any synovial fluid in the joints; it is as if that his sentences were threatening to crack and splinter at each punctuation mark; it is the sort of prose that it is time to put away. Noirot de Sauw does little himself, very little. He quotes documents relentlessly, puts all his notes in place and stitches his sentences together. Then he signs the patchwork and sends it pompously to all the academies, before which he bows down to the ground. It is said, in fact, that he has academic pretensions; may God protect all the academics there have ever been and are to come.

Sad, sad! Envious, jealous and cantankerous towards everyone—sad, sad! In sum, he is a type; he is pardoned out of love of science.

Abbé Omnish is another type; but you know him. Is there anyone on the surface of the world who does not know him? A good colleague and genuinely knowledgeable, he has few rivals, if any.

I shall come back to the debates, from which I have allowed myself to be distracted while contemplating the handsome and sanctimonious face of Seringuier.

Mr. Newbold: "The floor is Mr. Liesse's."

Mr. Liesse: "I only a have a few words to say, Mr. President. Mr. Greenwight, in his remarkable dissertation, thought that we might obtain some clarification from the density of the aerolith. Matter must indeed be less condensed on Mars, and much more so on the Moon; that might be a very simple way of removing our satellite from the debate.

"I have, with the collaboration of Mr. Siemann, determined the density of several samples, including that of the silver found in the bolide. The figures are very similar to those we obtain with respect to terrestrial metals and minerals, but a little lower. It is as well to add, however, that the proportional density of these materials ought to be less than it is in reality; at any rate, it is too similar to permit the attribution of their origin to our satellite; the density of lunar rocks must be significantly lower, and, for reasons that Mr. Greenwight has argued very well, I have no hesitation in to remove the Moon from the debate."

Mr. Greenwight: "I hope I might be permitted to thank Mr. Liesse for his support, and to remark to the assembly that, far from surprising me, the discordances observed by my savant colleague regarding the density of the aerolith's substance only serve to reaffirm my first opinion. Indeed, the density of these materials was, at the time of their fall, lower than those of similar terrestrial substances, but they have crossed space, becoming more condensed in the process, then aggregated in obedience to new terrestrial forces, then further condensed by the cooling that has occurred between their arrival here and the present time. Why should it be surprising that their density has been relatively increased? The contrary would be more difficult to explain. What I wanted most of all, in asking Mr. Liesse to determine the density, was to remove the Moon from the question. Now, the question raised by Mr. Stek appears to me to be conclusively settled. The aerolith and its contents can only have descended, in theory, from the planet Mars; what remains to be explained is how. It is Mr. Owerght who wanted to take responsibility for this point and will, I am sure, clarify it with his usual talent."

Mr. Haughton: "Mr. President, I asked to speak several sessions ago, and I think that it would not be superfluous, before examining the possibility of the fall of an aerolith originating from another planet, to embark straight away on the most important question—in my opinion—of the development of creatures on the surface of the Earth and similar worlds. I should like, in that respect, to raise a few objections to Mr. Greenwight's opinion."

Mr. Newbold: "The floor is Mr. Haughton's, but I am bound to remind you, Gentlemen, that time is passing, and I recommend my colleagues to be as brief as possible."

Mr. Haughton: "Who says *creature*, gentlemen, says *life*. Now, what is life? For Mr. Greenwight, if I have understood correctly, life results from a given unified mass and a given quantity of motion. But if that were the case, gentlemen, what would prevent me from producing life? Am I not the master of the quantity of motion; can I not increase or diminish mass at will?

"Here is some matter, then some more matter; can I animate it? No, a thousand times no. I can produce chemical reactions, which will not continue by themselves and will extinguish themselves after a certain lapse of time. That is not the nature of life. And besides, if that were the case, we would see life becoming manifest from moment to moment, everywhere that matter is in contact with matter; spontaneous generation would produce it before our eyes all the time. There is none.

"Then again, why is there death after such a brief evolution of matter? Is it not obvious that the quantity of motion cannot have varied much in so short a time? Besides, individual succeeds individual, and what kills one animates another; there are anomalies and contradictions here that force me to reject the definition made in advance by the savant astronomer. No, life is not a reaction."

Mr. Ziegler: "I shall take the liberty of interrupting my illustrious colleague; I share Mr. Greenwight's ideas up to a point, and I cannot let Mr. Haughton's negations pass without reply. I am even more insistent about this because, in another arena—in France—no other academician, in a dispute that has last several years, has dared to put forward the opinion that I oppose to Mr. Haughton. My honorable colleague's cause is defended artfully in Paris by Messieurs Pasteur, Milne-Edwards, Balard, etc., etc., and mine, or similar ones, by provincial professors: Messieurs Pouchet, Joly and Musset. Why, in the Institut de France, even though several academicians have a fixed opinion on the subject, has no one raised his voice in favor of heterogenesis? [47]

---

[47] Parville: "Mr. Ziegler presumably did not know at this time that Monsieur E. Frémy, Professor of Chemistry at the Museum and the Ecole Polytechnique, and member of the Académie, had generously put his laboratory at the disposal of the heterogenists, when all other doors were closed to them. We do not know M. Frémy's opinions on spontaneous generation, but we can make the observation to Mr. Ziegler that and academician of the Institut de France had dared to extend a hand to the heterogenists when, not only were they not defended, but were still rejected from all professions by orthodox science." This initial reference here is to Edmond Frémy (1814-1894). The people ranked on the conventional side of the debate alongside Louis Pasteur (1822-1895) are Henri Milne-Edwards (1800-1885) and Antoine-Jérome Balard (1802-1876). Pasteur's great rival in the debate regarding spontaneous generation, Félix-Archimede Pouchet (1800-1872), was the director of the Museum of Natural History in Rouen; Nicolas Joly and Charles Musset collaborated on papers in support of his thesis.

"I ask you not to follow that example and, although I am cutting out a path that is entirely new to you, I ask permission fully to explain my thinking. What we are all seeking, gentlemen, if not the truth? We must work together, each contributing his stone to the edifice.

"Evidently, matter added to matter cannot produce life in every instance, but I dare to assert that the necessary and sufficient conditions lie in that juxtaposition. Organic bodies are bodies whose material elements are susceptible to being stimulated by the quantity of motion normally originating from the World itself or from the Sun; these bodies enter into harmonic vibration; they become animated; they live—and the reactions thus produced are perpetuated for a given time, which it will be necessary to define in due course.

"As for the material elements of organic bodies, note this: they are always formed of various mineral materials, dependent on the milieu in which they are placed, and are invariably wholly or partly made up of certain fixed components: carbon, nitrogen, hydrogen and oxygen.

"You deny that uniting matter with matter suffices to determine life, but do you not see an implicit reply in that continual juxtaposition of four substances: carbon, nitrogen, hydrogen, oxygen? Can you not perceive clearly that only certain varieties of matter, certain aggregations and certain compounds have the ability to constitute living bodies? Can it not be admitted that, if you know how to place them in the presence of the required conditions, you would produce life?

"Right! A creature can only be formed out of one substance, one specifically-defined substance among the innumerable materials of nature, which can become a creature—but you refuse to see that as the first clue!

114

Logic instructs you at least to admit a doubt and forbids you to cut such a difficulty question short so quickly."

Mr. Newbold: "Let us not forget the interplanetary habitant, gentlemen."

Mr. Ziegler: "Yes, Mr. President; I'm moving on.

"Whenever you find yourself in the presence of material aggregations too dense as yet to be excited by the quantity of motion received from the planet, you will only have inert bodies before your eyes, incapable of entering into a harmonic vibration with that motion, incapable of perpetuating that force for a certain time, incapable of living. That is inorganic nature.

"On the other hand, if you have before you aggregations sufficiently dense, mobile enough to store the motion and perpetuate it for a certain time, just as a string moved by a bow continues to vibrate when the effort has ceased, you will see those aggregations that were inert just now born, developing and living. That is organic nature.

"Now, is this a mere hypothesis, a dream? If so, why do we only ever find the same molecules associated, the same atomic aggregations: carbon, nitrogen, hydrogen, oxygen? You see, gentlemen, that certain molecules alone, in invariable composition, like to come together. They alone are capable of receiving and transmitting the motion. Is it not necessary to conclude, whether we like it or not, that with them alone can life be produced? The proposition is therefore true that appropriate matter, excited by an appropriate quantity of motion, is a necessary and sufficient condition of the emergence of life. From that comes this definition: organic substance is merely the matter susceptible to harmonic excitation in the presence of the quantity of motion freely available at the surface of the globe.

"Life is merely the release of the quantity of internal motion originally stored in matter and perpetuated by the quantity of external motion. Life therefore depends on the initial aggregation of matter and the environment in which it finds itself."

Mr. Haughton: "Does Mr. Ziegler extend this opinion, not merely to organic matter—which is to say, to the substance susceptible to increase and decrease which constitutes living beings—but to living beings themselves: to animals and vegetables?"

Mr. Ziegler: "Most certainly; the law applies universally. Mr. Greenwight has said on his own authority that constellations and worlds supercharged with quantity of motion are in an embryonic state. As that quantity of motion diminishes, worlds age; when it is nullified, they die. I have only to repeat his statement for organic nature. The excited matter is aggregated in various combinations.

"The fall of these innumerable atoms one upon another for each little body, however infinitesimal it is, produces a great quantity of motion.[48] The release of that

---

[48] Parville: "Modern physicists do indeed attribute every chemical combination to an actual collision of atoms or molecules. Everyone knows that the impact of a bullet striking a target determines the heat generated, because the annihilated motion is transformed into heat. Heat and motion are, in effect, different manifestations of a single cause. Now, if a chemical combination generates heat, it is precisely because of the impact of molecules upon one another. The combustion of carbon in oxygen is a phenomenon of the same order as a body falling to Earth; a diamond that burns in oxygen only catches fire by virtue of the fall of oxygen atoms upon it. One could calculate the heat produced if one knew the velocity of atoms, their mass and their rate of progress.

quantity of internal motion, slowed down every day by the quantity of external motion, just as the cooling of the Earth is slowed by the radiation of the Sun, determines the different phases of life.

"The energy of the spring that releases it is the vital force; thus you pass necessarily from youth to old age, and when the quantity of internal motion is finally exhausted, and the external excitation is insufficient to maintain equilibrium, Death follows.

"The molecular aggregations still subsist thereafter, just as the worlds still remain in their solid state after the completion of their cooling, but when the molecules have finished vibrating in unison with the molecules of neighboring bodies and there is no more tendency to aggregate, organic bodies become disorganized in their turn, like old worlds in space. The molecules, like the

---

"The observation might be made that the heat produced by the impact of a body falling to Earth is out of all proportion to that produced in the previous experiment of atomic impacts. The response is simple. To establish a comparison, it is necessary to put identical conditions in place. Atoms of carbon and oxygen hurl themselves upon one another from a large relative distance. Let us, therefore, imagine lifting up a body far enough from the Earth for attraction to become almost negligible, as is the case with atoms; calculation will then demonstrate that the speed of the fall will be such that it generates twice as much heat as the combustion of an equal weight of pure carbon. One cannot, therefore, any longer be astonished by the temperature produced by the impact of atoms upon one another.

"The aggregation of an ensemble of atoms thus generates a great deal of heat and motion. That is the origin of life, when the atoms are appropriate and the quantity of motion of the surrounding body is susceptible to harmonic stimulation."

interplanetary atoms, resume their liberty to enter into new combinations somewhere else. Such is the cycle of life.

"Mr. Haughton asks me how I give birth thus to vegetables and animals. I have demonstrated the generation of tissue, the embryonic cells of all organic substance; the ensemble will be born from the details, the creature from constituent parts. But the session is well advanced; with the agreement of the assembly, I shall postpone the development of this thesis until tomorrow.

LETTER X

The genesis of living beings. The first organisms on Earth. Rudimentary vegetables. The law of formation and reproduction. The first animals. A few lines by Lavoisier. The solidarity of living beings. Species. Varieties. From which terrain did human beings originate? Such a ground, such an animal. On size. The epoch of large animals.

Mr. Ziegler still has the floor.

Mr. Ziegler: "Gentlemen, if the details that I introduced yesterday are still present in your memories, I think I can give you some assistance with respect to the genesis of creatures, as Mr. Greenwight has unfolded before to the genesis of worlds.

"In the beginning, the quantity of motion of our globe was too great to permit any juxtaposition of organic elements. When it became small enough to permit their association and aggregation, the organic molecules were combined, and produced the first rudimentary organisms—organisms that would have been invisible to us, so small and imperceptible were they, had we been capable of existing on the world's surface at that time. What were these organisms? We shall be careful in defining them. What were they! Masses of molecules that, in combination, had—by virtue of that very fact—condensed a certain quantity of motion. That aggregation, excited by external motion, was capable of increasing by the adjunction of new molecules, by virtue of an exchange with other neighboring materials—which gave rise to birth, life, and then, after the release of all the motion, death. Thus the most rudimentary organisms were born, in the infancy of our planet; they were doubtless compounded in abundance almost everywhere, covering the surface of the globe.

"But these little bodies, these tiny elementary cells tossed about randomly in the milieu of an atmosphere charged with gas, ended up falling back on to the solid surface; they found new elements of aggregation there, and the majority, extracting organic materials from the ground, drew them into their evolution and transformed themselves into more complex organisms.[49] Thus the

---

[49] This notion of self-transformation is central to the idea of evolution developed by Charles Darwin's most famous predecessor, Jean-Baptiste de Monet, Chevalier de Lamarck (1744-1829), in his *Philosophie zoologique* (1809), which proposed that the vital force which Lamarck imagined to be the essence of life had an innately progressive element. In his philosophy, every organism is constantly striving to improve itself by enhancing its adaptation to its environment; the notion that acquired characteristics had to be inherited—which is now seen as the aspect of Lamarckism that contrasts it crucially with the modern synthesis of Darwinism and genetics—was a mere corollary of this fundamental assumption. Mr. Ziegler—his opinion clearly endorsed Parville—remains a diehard Lamarckian, apparently considering natural selection as unworthy of mention, let alone serious consideration. French evolutionary theory continued in this same nationalistic vein for some time; Henri Bergson (1859-1941) eventually revived and repackaged the idea of an innately progressive *élan vital* in *L'évolution creatrice* (1907) in calculated opposition to the seemingly-irresistible tide of Darwinist conviction. Ziegler and Parville are thus steering a course between the polarized opinions of Pouchet and Pasteur, attempting an eclectic selection of their ideas. Given this, Ziegler's eventual abrupt modification of the apparent tendency of his view—which even Parvillle calls a "volte-face"—is not at all surprising.

primitive organic molecule went on, constantly and successively complicating itself, sometimes taking force and density into its adjunction along with organic molecules. Such is the origin of vegetables. Forms multiplied increasingly, from the cell and the elementary tissue to multiple tissues. It was, first and foremost, a matter of mass, time and the quantity of internal and external motion.

"Do you imagine that one of these masses of organic molecules, in the presence of new masses, would have been able to increase permanently and grow indefinitely by juxtaposition and combination? No, gentlemen, the primitive vegetable, the rudimentary cell, could not grow infinitely. Its life depends on its quantity of motion, and its quantity of motion is finite.

"When the developable surface of a cellule has become sufficiently large, by virtue of the adjunction of neighboring molecules, under the action of external forces—the world's own heat and solar radiation—an equilibrium will be established between its superficial diminution and its vital release; the organic element will no longer be able to increase. Consider this curious mechanism, though. It is the surface that makes the individual waste away; the quantity of motion insufficient to keep it alive in its new state also concentrates its efforts at a single point. A new center of action forms, of newly-aggregated molecules; a new individual appears. Worlds are constantly-varying centers of action; these rudimentary vegetables are also centers of aggregation, incessantly transmutable. It is thus that the primitive cell reproduces itself, endlessly, by fission, fragmentation, budding, etc.

"One might suppose that there is a continual loss of quantity of motion in the death and birth of each organic element, but there is not, for the forced aggregation of new molecules condenses new forces every time.

"With regard to these infinitely tiny rudimentary individuals, it is evident that we ought to find them in al the eras of the existence of our planet, for as long as the conditions of temperature permit organic molecules to exist. They form wherever and whenever the physical elements of their existence are not lacking, or they reproduce by fractionation.

"From the preceding argument, it seems to me, contrary to the opinion of Mr. Haughton, that if one puts the organic elements together, in the desired quantity—if you expose them to an appropriate heat and, especially, light, and to the desired humidity and electrical conditions—you will produce their association, and inevitably constitute creatures capable of living, nourishing themselves and reproducing themselves—which are, in consequence, vegetables by definition.[50]

---

[50] Parville: "Let us summarize in this regard what Mr. Tyndall, professor of physics at the Royal Institution, said in one of his excellent lectures: The Sun, which is to say, the source of heat, of quantity of motion, is the universal hearth of organic and animal life. It *works* to fabricate plants and animals. It has been said that the atoms of different substances, when they combine, fall upon one another in the manner of a body falling to Earth. In the same way that one can lift a body off the ground, one can separate atoms that have combined. Thus, the universally familiar carbonic acid gas results from the fall of molecules of oxygen on molecules of carbon. This compound is gaseous and spreads into the atmosphere. It can disappear, when one draws apart its constituent molecules and renders intact the atoms of carbon and oxygen that formed it. Carbonic acid, in fact, furnishes vegetables with the carbon that enters into their make-up. Solar light separates the atoms, liberating

"The vegetable cell is distinct from the animal cell; although it has the same origin, its molecular grouping is different. Agate, japer and amethyst are only forms of flint, but their molecules are variously combined; it is

---

the oxygen that serves animal life, and introduces the carbon into the constitutive aggregation of the ligneous fibre.

"Also, when a ray of sunlight penetrates a forest, the quantity of heat that will be rendered by the ray will not be exactly equal to the quantity received. A portion will have been employed in fabricating trees. It should be noted that the solar ray only excites the organic molecules and remains insufficient to act mechanically on inorganic molecules; here again the principle proposed by Ziegler is perceptible.

"Is not the fact marvellous in itself? Consider that luminous ray which slips coquettishly from branch to branch through the verdure. Perhaps you think it good for nothing—what a mistake! Good for nothing! But it is what makes the tree; it is what makes the forest in the midst of which you are strolling, that charming bush, those little birds that are pecking within it, seemingly thanking it with their joyful song. Oh, if poets knew everything that is beautiful and sublime in the golden ray that illuminates their souls, they would never dare rhyme again and would fall silent, mute with admiration before the grandeur of the spectacle and the incomparable splendour of the work—but poets claim that science and the poem are poles apart, alas!"

The reference is to John Tyndall (1820-1893), one of many distinguished scientists who carried forward the tradition of public lectures at the Royal Institution while further developing the ideas of their founder, Michael Faraday. Tyndall had not yet published a book in 1865, when this note was written—Parville was presumably present at the actual lectures—but he went on to establish a considerable career as a popularizer as well as a researcher; if the final comment in Parville's note was Tyndall's, it was probably a conscious echo of Robert Hunt's *Poetry of Science* (1848).

the same with the vegetable cell and the animal element. The anatomical rudiments were doubtless constituted at the same time as the vegetable rudiments, and the difference is still imperceptible today. Certain animals and certain vegetables are so similar that one cannot precisely identify the point at which the animal sequence ends, giving way to the vegetable sequence.

"Like the rudimentary vegetables, the first animal organisms, in extracting new materials from the bosom of the waters, the air and the surface of the ground, became more complex and increased in dimension. Like the vegetables, they were obliged to grow no further beyond a certain limit, and their death led to the birth of new individuals. With regard to the duration of their life, it is evidently proportional to the initial quantity of motion stored by molecular aggregation and the surface of each creature. It is therefore not considerable; reproduction has to manifest itself very energetically. Life and death overtake these organisms with an extreme rapidity.

"The primitive organisms must have existed alone for a considerable time, some in the atmosphere, some on the solid surface, and others in the seas. Then, when calmer conditions prevailed on the globe, and sediments began to be deposited, the organisms became more numerous and more varied. The vegetable cells found materials for assimilation all around them, in abundance. The animal cells augmented themselves at the expense of the vegetable cells and the mineral substances of the atmosphere and the seas. The exchanges multiplied, forms becoming more varied, and the first species corresponding to the earliest ages of the globe gradually appeared.

"Each species thus formed inevitably perpetuated itself from the time of its creation to a more distant epoch. In effect, an organism is a center of action, it is stored force; death does not come until that force is exhausted, but the external forces—heat, light, etc.—which stimulate the release of each individual life also work to accumulate within it materials borrowed from the environment into which it is plunged.

"Now, in order that these forces can stimulate the vital release, it is absolutely necessary to admit that they are capable of doing exactly the same work; otherwise, there would be an arrest; life would not have appeared. The external forces can, therefore, work to group new molecules and are capable of determining by that aggregation a quantity of life equal to that possessed by the individual. This new aggregation permits the formation of a germ, the embryo of an individual similar to the preceding one—and thus it continues.

"Nevertheless, the external forces are subject to an incessant but imperceptible diminution. Inevitably therefore, the quantity of life that they accumulate in each germ will also diminish. At length, the species will perish. That is one of the regular and imperceptible causes of the extinction of species. The lifespan of each individual, as we have said, depends on its mass and its developable surface; it is the same with the power of reproduction.

"I have no need to observe that these considerations find further confirmation every day. Place a seed or an organism already in motion in an environment deprived of heat and light, and you will never, ever see life arise or perpetuate itself. Moreover, gentlemen, I must render justice here to the founder of chemistry, a Frenchman we all admire, the great Lavoisier. I found this memorable passage in his writings, which says it all:

"'Organization, feeling, spontaneous movement and life only exist on the surface of the Earth and in the places exposed to light. One might say that the flame of Prometheus' torch was a philosophical expression, which had not escaped the ancients. Without light, nature was without life; it was dead an inanimate. A benevolent God, in bringing light, has spread organization, feeling and thought over the surface of the Earth.'

"These words will remain an eternal expression of truth."

(Prolonged applause.)

Mr. Newbold: "We are listening with the most lively interest, Mr. Ziegler, but I am forced to recall that we are incessantly straying from the question. These digressions, interesting as they may be, are not advancing the solution of the problem. Mr. Ziegler might care to recall that we have been meeting for ten days, and we still do not know what conclusions to draw regarding the inhabitant of the planet Mars."

Mr. Ziegler: "Mr. President, I shall be finished soon. If the assembly will authorize me to do it, I shall complete my task."

("Yes! Yes! Yes!")

"To continue: only vegetables, gentlemen, possess the faculty of drawing organic and inorganic molecules directly from the soil; they make organic matter directly. That is because of the simplicity of the aggregations which constitute them. Animals do not have that privilege; they can only grow at the expense of organic substance, vegetable or animal. Vegetables thus precede animals in creation. That is very remarkable, it seems to me, and is a very good indicator of the distance that separates the two kinds of organisms. One elaborates that which the other subsequently absorbs.

"On sees here, from the outset, the appearance of an immutable law of nature. All organization proceeds incessantly by ascendant degrees, from the simple to the complex, the first creation serving the next, and so on.

"An animal cannot extract the primitive elements of growth from its immediate surroundings, since it needs them to be subjected to an initial elaboration. It is therefore necessary for it to be able to displace itself. In the beginning, this necessity of displacement would have forced rudimentary organisms to fashion themselves for movement, and that faculty would have increased with the variety of nutrients drawn from every direction. Thus the animal would have been alone among natural bodies in having the ability to carry out external labor: a great concession which gifted it with all its superiority. That privilege, we repeat, small at first—very small—would have increased continually.

"We would therefore have, in the first epochs, creatures that could only displace themselves with difficulty—then, successively, animals better and better conformed for locomotion.

"Reciprocal material affinities would give birth to the qualities of each individual, since instinct is the dominant character of every species. It is perfectly certain that the animals and vegetables of every period are not only dependent on one another, but that each one is dependent on many others.

"A mathematician will say that it is the combination of the variables that determine the solution of an equation. When the equation—which is to say, the external forces—changes, the variables—which is to say, the species—inevitably change too.

"If you will permit me, gentlemen, to direct your meditations towards a great principle that appears to govern the evolution of matter, I will define it thus: 'Every molecular grouping tends to produce a similar molecular grouping.'

"The force that escapes from a given aggregation tends to produce, harmonically, the same number of atoms and to create similar molecules. That is why, gentlemen, the more sediments deposit themselves numerously on the terrestrial surface, the more substances group themselves and complicate themselves, and the more organisms group themselves and complicate themselves. You will find their structure becoming increasingly complicated and dependent on neighboring materials, the atmosphere, the seas and the land; their organs, their organs putting themselves in immediate relation with their needs. Fish conform themselves to live in the sea, birds in the air, mammals on the surface of the land.

"Each species, as we have said, cannot exist indefinitely. It is easy to calculate the duration of its existence. It has been born, in effect, under the stimulus of external forces acting on definitive molecular aggregations. The species is thus intimately linked to variations of external forces—heat, light, etc.—and consequently to variations in the substances of the globe.

"The organisms formed by the most rudimentary molecules perpetuate themselves for the longest times; on the contrary, because the most complex molecules vary their groupings much more quickly, the most creatures higher in the scale perpetuate themselves for shorter periods.

"A species will inevitably become extinct when it no longer encounters molecules similar to those which form it, and when the external forces become insufficient to determine its stimulation.

"In ordinary language, every time a geological revolution has modified the environment, the species have changed; they transformed themselves, although the transition would be less evident because the previous animals and vegetables, and the ground itself, would have become more complex and more variable.

"Thus, one can translate the preceding argument by saying that the first organisms, scarcely modified, will perpetuate themselves through almost al the ages of the Earth; that vegetables and animals, more elevated in the ascendant scale, can only perpetuate themselves for a limited time, their origin and their extinction essentially depending on the physical and geological environment; they therefore differ generally in each geological phase—much more so, if the cataclysm that rearranges the materials of the terrestrial surface is of greater magnitude itself, but much less, on the other hand, when the changes are more insignificant.[51]

---

[51] Parville: "While Mr. Ziegler was imparting these new views, a knowledgeable French traveller, Monsieur Trémaux, was bringing strong arguments in favour of the same thesis to the Institut de France, and the two naturalists were certainly unaware of the analogy of pinion that bound them together.

"M. Trémaux, in a remarkable and oft-remarked series of memoirs, had proposed this law: it is the geological and physical environment that makes the species. The least advanced human beings belong to the most ancient terrains, and also to the least favourable climates. Inversely, the most advanced human beings belong to the lands in which the least space offers the greatest variety of terrain, allowing the predominance of the most recent, and—again as a corollary—to the most favourable climate and other secondary causes.

"Do we not find in this simple law the key to the divergences that separate the unitary school and the partisans of the diversity of the origin of species? Fixity, variability, degeneration—the formula holds in every case. Go to live in modern terrains, improvement; remain in place, fixity; settle primitive regions, degeneration. Is that not the scale of naturalists, with its steps taken upwards or downwards?

"M. Trémaux has accumulated proofs. We shall cite a few examples. The Sudan has rather wretched inhabitants. Let us look at its geological constitution. Primitive terrains almost everywhere, with gold mines. Australia, so rich in mines, is formed almost entirely of eruptive rocks; its population is very degraded and even blacker than their neighbors even though they are outside the tropics. In southern Africa, the Bechuans and the Bakaas visited by Dr. Livingstone are scarcely favored; their land is constituted by Silurian rocks and mountains of black basalt. In the valley of the Zambesi the soil becomes fertile; the populations are ameliorated. The geological map of Europe shows us that the largest surface of primitive terrain corresponds to Lapland, which also has the most inferior people. On the other hand, are not the most favored countries France, Italy, Greece, the eastern part of Spain and the north-east of England?

"The peoples of the southern hemisphere are inferior to the corresponding peoples of the northern hemisphere; in the same way, the inhabitants of most islands are less advanced than others. It is sufficient, in fact, to cast one's eyes over a geological map to observe that there again the regions under consideration belong to the most ancient terrains.

"Let us remind ourselves of a fact perceived by Geoffroy Saint-Hilaire, that the degree of domestication of animals is proportional to the degree of civilization of the humans who possess them. It is obvious, in fact, that humans and animals living on the same ground are necessarily advanced or retarded to the same degree, according to the geological formations.

"Such is the terrain, such are its human beings."

"With the variety of terrains comes the variety of species; with their multiplicity, the superiority and elevation of individuals.

"You see, gentlemen, that I am not side-stepping anything. I formally deny that creation was the work of a day; I strongly oppose the opinion that gives birth all of a piece to the various species that populate the Earth.

"Many scientists, especially in Europe, affirm that the germs of all the animals that exist, have existed or will exist, were created at the beginning of time, only commencing their evolution successively, in their turn. That is absolutely contrary to reason and to the profound study of biological phenomena.

"No, gentlemen, species and individuals, descended from the primitive organic molecule, pass, like the globe itself, through distinct phases. A species is born, grows and dies, like an individual; it is a whole that is subject to differentiation.

"Like the globe, though, like the planetary system to which we belong, every species, in losing its life, is destined to commence the generation of a new species; it is a simple matter of the transmission of force.

"Cast a glance over our epoch; you will see contemporary species very similar to preceding species. There is already transformation. Our contemporary animals and vegetables will undergo transition, by imperceptible degrees into new animals and other vegetables.

"The end of the existence of our species will correspond to the generation of successors, in correspondence

---

The references are to the architect and amateur ethnographer Pierre Trémaux (1818-1895), who published an elaborate account of his travels in Africa in 1862, and the famous naturalist Étienne Geoffroy Saint-Hilaire (1805-1861).

with the external forces of the epoch, with its geological environments. That is inevitable; the materials and the workman change; it is necessary that the work is transformed.

"No one is any longer astonished to see a type of rock stratum characterized by its flora and fauna, since that is exactly what regulated the evolution of organisms during the lapse of time that it has revealed.

"With respect to the distinct varieties that each species shows, according to what we have just summarized, anyone can see at first glance that they are just as intimately related to geological and physical environments. It is the soil and the ambient environment that fabricate, chemically and physically, the species and the individual.[52]

"The further the revolution of the globe proceeds, the more creatures will advance by imperceptible degrees, for the combinations of matter will become more difficult and rarer, and the species, in consequence, will be more and more dependent on one another.

"This remark also suffices to make it evident that species, after succeeding one another with great rapidity and variety, ought to begin to become more stable and less amenable to transformation.

---

[52] Parville: "We find confirmation of this in what we see every day. Do not the species of our contemporary trees vary with latitude—which is to say, with external forces, with terrains; which is to say, with the materials of the globe? Who does not know, besides, that certain species can only live in given latitudes? The external forces are, in fact, insufficient in the cold regions or too excessive in the hot regions to permit life to develop."

"Not only has the structure of creatures been modified, but also their stature. Is it not perfectly obvious that it must have increased with the variety of disposable materials? The stored force has become greater and the possible growth of each individual more considerable.

"It seems that we have passed the maximum and that, as the exterior forces are decreasing more quickly than the variety of combinations is increasing, the stature of species is now diminishing.

"It is unnecessary to add that, in each phase, the largeness of a creature still depends on the latitude and has always increased from the pole to the equator. Numerous observations have always proved, in fact, that, in conformity with these deductions, the largest animals are always encountered in the equatorial regions. I shall terminate these considerations, in view of the late hour, on Monday, if the assembly will permit."

LETTER XI

How we come to life. Vital release. Means of measuring it. Why the vegetable that grows in the dark weighs less than the seed that produced it. The maximum of life. Duration of existence. Mr. Ziegler disagrees with M. Flourens. Human longevity. Why do vegetables awaken in spring? Does man create his likeness? Machines for manufacturing creatures. The transmission of organic force. The Creator.

Mr. Ziegler: "Several members of the commission wanted to raise objections to what I said yesterday, on Sunday; I fear that the physiologists have not entirely grasped my meaning, and I ask, gentleman, to say something further about the origin of life. Others have only seen my explanation as a materialist thesis without consequences; I feel compelled to enlighten the former and reassure the latter.

"I repeat at this point the fundamental principle already cited: every molecular aggregation tends to engender a similar molecular aggregation.

"The germ, gentlemen, is a definite and elaborate molecular aggregation produced by organic forces in function. Take a germ, a seed or an egg: if you do not put this one or that one in the required physical conditions, you will get nothing from it, absolutely nothing from one or the other. But plant the seed in a suitable environment, of a sort in which it can find around it similar molecules to adjoin to itself, and you will soon see vital activity develop and the seed transform itself into a plant.

"Was the seed or the embryo, then, before its excitation by external forces, a raw, inert, inorganic entity? No, gentlemen; it was an aggregation of organic molecules not in possession of the quantity of motion required to adjoin similar molecules to itself. It was an incomplete creation, only awaiting an excess of force to transform itself. I have said that two conditions must be fulfilled before the seed can produce the plant: sufficient external forces, and the required elements of aggregation. Here, gentlemen, is an immediate verification.

"Let us suppress, only partially, the external forces; let us, for example, place the seed in total darkness, and let us keep the elements of aggregation. Life, we have said, is the release of a stored force. Now, let us release the force stored in the seed; as we have suppressed the major part of the excitatory force, evidently the life will be very short; new molecules cannot be grouped around the old; when the quantity of motion stored is exhausted, the organism will die.

"Now consider this: here is a seed; we have placed it in the Sun; it has germinated; then we have shut it up in a dark room. Solar excitation has given it life; the suppression of that force does not take it away. It is necessary to wait for the stored force to be exhausted; the plant will therefore continue to live, and the larger its embryo was, the longer it will live. Eventually, we shall see it wither, and then die. The plant will have exhausted all the force stored in its embryo.

"Here, set out very simply, is the notion of the release of vital force. If an organism lives for a long time, it is incontestably due to the force that gives birth to the gradual aggregation of new molecules.

"We should add that the loss of the force has inevitably led to the loss of molecules and that a plant that has sprouted in the dark weighs less than the seed that produced it. This seems paradoxical, gentlemen, but I have planted seeds, having weighed them, then, when the plants that sprouted in the darkness were on the point of dying, I weighed them again. The loss can be as much as 50%.[53]

"By contrast, leave the seed, the excitatory forces and the molecules of aggregation in place, and you will see the plant sprout and gain weight incessantly. In this instance, in fact, the germ, far from losing quantity of motion, gains it incessantly. The molecules no longer escape combination; they enter into it. Life is thus augmented within the organism, along with its weight; in this fashion, every time the external forces increase, you will observe an increase of vital energy and a new augmentation of weight. The external forces increase every spring, when you also see buds appear and stems spring up more numerously. The phenomenon is quite simple.

"Will the plant grow indefinitely, then, and will its life increase incessantly? No, gentlemen; as with everything else in the universe, there is a maximum, and, once

---

[53] Parville: "This fact has been explained recently by a French academician, Monsieur Boussingault. It is sufficient to observe that the germ is not the seed. A seed that has germinated in darkness evidently loses its weight, but the plant gains less weight than the seed loses. To explain the anomaly it was necessary to compare the embryo to the plant and it was seen that the plant weighed more than the embryo. This takes nothing away from Mr. Ziegler's reasoning. The seed nourishes and feeds the embryo, and when its materials are used up, the plant dies." The reference is to the agricultural chemist Jean-Baptiste Boussingault (1802-1887), whose name is misrendered as "Bisingault" in Parville's text.

it is passed, life is progressively lost, eventually disappearing entirely.

"Life follows an ascendant curve for as long as the external forces prevail over the force of internal release and the organism gains in weight, but equilibrium is inevitably reached; the eliminatory internal force, to use the term customary in physiology, ends up by equaling the assimilatory external force. At that moment, the plant is neither gaining nor losing; life has attained its maximum; it will henceforth diminish.

"And indeed, the external force can no longer produce further aggregation; it is entirely employed in stimulating and maintaining the molecules that have been aggregated. The stored force alone is free to act; in accordance with what has already been said, we can see that it is precisely equal to the external force that has built the organism. It has become so by virtue of the successive aggregation of molecules; it will gradually diminish by virtue of a successive and slow disaggregation.

"More powerful now than the equilibrated external force, it will expend more material than the other cam import; it will make a gradual but incessant loss; the plant will lose weight. It is true that each new aggregation brings a new quantity of life, but, because a part of the motion engendered is employed in exciting the added molecule, there is an overall subtraction of force and a diminution.

"Now, the external force is relatively infinite in quantity; the interior force, by contrast, is essentially finite. Being incessantly lost, it is inevitable that it will be reduced to nothing and that the organism will die. As this loss progresses, the molecules draw nearer to one another; the plant's tissue becomes more compact; it grows old.

"Some among you, gentlemen, will already have perceived the important consequence that emerges from the preceding facts.

"The vital force equals, at its maximum, the level of the external force that has produced it; is that not as much as to say that, if you double the time necessary for an organism to complete its development, you will have doubled the normal duration of its life? Is it not as much as to say that the rapidity of an individual's growth will decrease incessantly from birth to the maximum of life, and, conversely, that the rapidity of loss will increase incessantly from the maximum of life until death?

"A given organism, therefore, will exhale more carbonic acid in its old age than in its youth , and that gives us a means of determining the age of an individual.

"If, gentlemen, you need to measure the duration of an organism's existence, you should have a measuring-device ready to hand. Measure it and, when it has attained its full development, it will be sufficient to double its age to calculate its normal lifespan. These facts, which are confirmed every day, lend considerable support to the theory that I have had the honor of explaining to you."

Mr. Newbold: "The inhabitant of Mars, Mr. Ziegler! What about the inhabitant of Mars? Will we ever get around to it?"

Mr. Ziegler: "I've finished, Mr. President—or very nearly. I have briefly shown you birth, life and death in the vegetable kingdom. A few words now about the animal."

Mr. Williamson: "He's off again—he'll fill an entire book…"

138

Mr. Ziegler, without paying any heed to interruptions: "Firstly, gentlemen, between an egg and a seed, there is the greatest and the most complete analogy. Judge for yourself:

Eggs	Seeds
Albumin	Albumin
Gross matter	Gross matter
Milk sugar, glucose	Starch, dextrine giving glucose
Sulfur, phosphorus	Sulfur, phosphorus
Calcium phosphate	Calcium phosphate
Water in large proportion	Water in large proportion
--	Cellulose

"The composition is almost identical. Cellulose must exist in the egg; it will be discovered there when someone takes the trouble to look for it.[54] As with the seed, it requires determined physical conditions to excite motion among the animal molecules. Without heat, the egg remains inert.

"The development of an animal proceeds like that of a plant; instead of extracting unelaborated nutriments it will seek out substances already prepared which, while permitting its growth, augment its vital force. It imports material incessantly from without. As with the plant, there will be a necessary terminus to that increase.

"There will be an augmentation of the individual so long as the vital force is not equal to the force that determines the aggregation of ingested materials, but, when that limit is attained, there will be more elimination than fixation of new elements, and life will diminish imperceptibly. Here again it is not necessary to assume that the acquired materials will disappear rapidly.

---

[54] This assumption turned out to be erroneous; cellulose is a definitive constituent of plant tissue.

"In whatever fashion, the vital force exhales materials; by virtue of that fact, it breaks the equilibrium, and the external force enters into a new relationship with it, in which the former prevails over the latter and there is a further subtraction every day, until the complete extinction of all vital motion.

"The law of the duration of existence that holds true for plants must hold true for animals. Every individual can determine the normal length of its life by doubling the number of years that is necessary for it to attain its full development. If a man ceases to grow at forty, it is because he will not live longer than eighty...and a few more years to take account of the time when the organism remains stationary. The man who does not acquire his full development until he is 50 will live to be 100.[55]

---

[55] Parville: "Mr. Ziegler's opinion is completely at odds with that of French physiologists. For Monsieur Flourens, the growth of an animal will be complete when the epiphyses are fixed to the bones. In man that is at 20 years. It is therefore necessary, in the reckoning of the celebrated author, to multiply the duration of growth by five to calculate the lifespan. A horse grows, according to him, for four or five years; its lifespan is 20 to 25, etc. Mr. Ziegler undoubtedly means by the duration of growth the entire time in which the animal does not decrease. On that basis, he might well be right, and it would be sufficient to double rather than quintuple that duration to calculate the real existence."

The reference is to the physiologist Pierre-Jean-Marie Flourens (1794-1867). The calculations made by Ziegler and Flourens both lack merit, although—as Ziegler's and Parville's attempts to dismiss the equine exception clearly testify—Ziegler's is even less plausible than Flourens. Once the vitalist hypothesis was firmly rejected and physiologists stopped thinking in terms of a quantifiable life force, the

"It is very probable, too, that there is a relationship between the duration of existence and the time of gestation. Thus, in humans, the elaboration lasts nine months; in chickens, 21 days; in dogs, 65 days; in horses, 11 months, and the duration of their existence is, respectively, 90 years, eight years, 12 years and 20 years. If the horse has such a short lifespan, the cause must lie in the excessive work that it accomplishes; wild horses must live much longer.

"It is also appropriate to take the mass of the embryo into account here. It is reasonably certain that the duration of existence and the time of gestation depend greatly on these elements.

"This is another opportunity to observe the very remarkable influence of variations of external forces on the phenomena of life. When the intensity of these forces diminishes, it is clear, according to the preceding argument, that the vital force—which is entirely bound up with it—ought to diminish. That is, indeed, what happens.

"For the plant, is it not in spring that it seems visibly to awaken from an apparent death? The external forces increase, and the vital force too; the plant or tree puts forth new growth. Every rotation of the Earth upon its axis has a similar influence; during the night, there is a diminution of vital force; there is, so to speak, sleep; the plant exhales carbonic acid. The internal force, more powerful than the external force, expels materials. When the Sun rises the effect is reversed, the external force prevails and the plant, instead of losing, produces a profit on the oxygen that it absorbs.

---

whole question of making calculations of this sort became redundant.

"In the same way, the animal feels itself reborn in spring. There is an increase in life. It also passes through an analogous phase every day. When the Sun disappears below the horizon, when light is lacking, it experiences an insatiable need for sleep. It manifests a curious reaction; the force that animates it seems to diminish, and, in fact, to diminish to the advantage of the force that reconstructs its tissues. One might think that, the external forces having partly disappeared, it no longer needs to effect external work; all the vital activity is concentrated inside the body that it repairs and grows. When the light returns, an inverse phenomenon is manifest, and it is, by contrast, the faculty of acting externally that prevails.

"All these facts find a very simple explanation, on which I do not want to dwell, in the considerations established in this session and the preceding one.

"You might like to note, gentlemen, that, in the final analysis, plants and animals are nothing but machines, receptors of force incessantly working upon matter. Now, here is a machine capable of a given force, a sum of quantity of movement, which is devoted, thanks to the astonishing phenomenon of reproduction, to generation: making a similar machine from component parts, creating a new sum of quantity of motion.

"Can two be made out of one? Can unity be created out of nothing? Be under no illusion, gentlemen, the act of generation is not production; it is not creation; it is a simple transformation of force, of that eternally transmissible force which has always existed, the immortal proof of the initial creation and of the Creator.

"A germ is only an aggregation of organic molecules combined by external forces. Now, external forces exist in indefinite quantity, as do organic molecules; an organism is only a machine that brings molecules together under the action of external forces; the germ does not borrow or take any of the vital force; it would necessarily be impoverished if external molecules could not replace those destined for the reproduction of the species. But we know that, until a given moment, molecules can enter into the organism and augment it.

"It is unnecessary to be astonished, therefore, in seeing a given sum of organic molecules produce a series of analogous sums; it only provides on each occasion, on its own account, an insignificant fraction of itself—and it only provides it, moreover, when its can extract a few superfluous units from itself without danger.

"Since reproduction depends on molecules that can be drawn from the reproductive creature and external forces, it is evident that it will take place primarily when those forces increase their intensity. This explains the need for love that animates animals in spring and awakens plants! In response to the greater excitation of the solar rays, plants and animals form new molecular agglomerations, which translate in visual terms into a bud or a fecund germ. The bud and the germ become new centers of action in their turn, destined to transmit the force that they already have and extract more from their surroundings.

"Such are, gentlemen, in their principles, the extremely simple and general laws that preside over evolution and the generation of species, and which govern the life of creatures. There only remains one last point one which to reassure several of my honorable colleagues; it is a matter of demonstrating that this admirable mechanism is not the expression of blind chance, that it does not lead to the notion of materialism, and that, on the contrary, it testifies in every respect to the omnipotence and the absolute necessity of a Creator."

(Cheers and applause from several benches.)

LETTER XII

An unexpected volte-face. *Where Mr. Ziegler becomes a spiritualist. Matter and the soul. Can thought activate material reactions? Mental and corporeal activity. On the existence of the soul. What a poor machine the body is! The influence of matter. The perfectibility of the individual and the perfectibility of impressions. Poor instruments, poor work. The theory of magnetism. How a soul can telegraph to another soul. Somnambulistic sleep. Magnetic influences. Mr. Haughton and M. Pasteur. Mr. Ziegler's conclusion.*

Mr. Newbold: "Gentlemen, several of our colleagues have received letters of recall; the debates are going on longer than we thought. It is, however, necessary to conclude. Mr. Ziegler has asked for the floor; after him, Mr. Owerght is scheduled. I shall be obliged to leave Paxton House myself in a few days; I therefore pray the Mr. Ziegler will be very brief, and I can only conserve his turn on that express condition."

Mr. Ziegler: "Thank you, Mr. President. A quarter of an hour will suffice for me to finish what I have to say."

From the journalists bench: "His quarter of an hour is bound to last several hours."

Mr. Ziegler: "I have been accused of favoring the most complete materialism by means of my theory. I claim a few more minutes of attention in order to exonerate myself.

"What have I done, gentlemen? I have shown that matter organizes itself under the influence of motion transmitted by matter; I have provided the explanation of these transformations. I have said subsequently that beings improve themselves as the materials of each planet become increasingly complex and varied. One might assume, indeed, that I would like to go further, arguing that intelligence becomes increasingly superior with the variety of material elements, and that, in consequence, intelligence depends exclusively on matter. It is important to draw a clear distinction.

"Yes, gentlemen, for me, intelligence depends on matter, but it is not matter that makes intelligence. It is necessary to distinguish the vital principle, the force that animates your body, from intelligence, from the soul. The vital principle belongs to the material world; intelligence is regulated by the material world, but does not belong to it. The vital principle is born and dies; the soul does not die.

"The vital principle arises entirely from matter: mass and quantity of motion, that is its formula. Without mass and without motion, there is no vital principle. Intelligence, by contrast, the faculty of thought, comes from the soul, from an element implicitly unknown, essentially divine.

"Why? Why does thought not arise spontaneously, exactly like the material reactions that produce the vital force? Gentlemen, it is very easy to prove the existence of a spiritual principle completely separate from the material world, and to provide clear evidence of its special nature.

"Has it not been demonstrated that life will increase its energy up to a certain limit, diminishing thereafter? This is a matter of the material reactions which produce the vital force. Now, if thought were also governed by the same evolutions, it would follow necessarily that intelligence would increase in the same proportion, subsequently to decrease in the same proportion.

"That is absolutely untrue. Although material decadence often does react upon—and, indeed, as we have shown, must react upon—the faculties of intelligence, intelligence very often remains tenacious and intact until the last moments of life. Thus, the production of thought, although linked to material reactions, cannot have the same origin as the vital force.

"Mental activity most often coincides with vital activity, but it is perfectly understandable that the soul profits from having a good deal of force to expend, and makes use of the power at its disposal. The soul, independent of the body, evidently directs the machine and makes use of it.[56]

"How—for I am obliged to go very quickly—is the intelligence dependent on the body? In absolutely the same fashion that a workman is dependent on an instrument. The soul can only communicate with the material world with the aid of a body; if the body is incomplete and badly-constructed, its material reactions insufficient, its vital principle insufficient, intelligence is limited—and you will understand that, gentlemen, with the greatest ease.

"The soul is connected via the body to the material world by means of organs of relation: the eye, the ear, the hands, etc. Now, the more complex and varied these

---

[56] Parville: "Let us add in support of this thesis that our body renews itself incessantly, that the one we shall have tomorrow is not the one we have today, and yet our *Self* remains exactly the same. If our ideas are modified as years go by, it is precisely because, as the constituent molecules vary, impressions must vary in consequence."

organs become, the more the intelligence will be impressed, the more sensation will multiply. Modify an organ, simplify its structure, and intelligence or instinct will be fatally depleted.

"How does an impression reach you? The impression is material in origin. It is a wave, a motion that strikes the ear, the eye the hand, the body. The stimulus is propagated by nerves to the brain. The impression is transmitted.

"The more different molecules there are, and the more different motions, as has been said, the more various sensations become in consequence. In order that all these motions should take effect, however, it is absolutely necessary that the organs which receive them should be susceptible to stimulation; it is necessary that their molecules should be as complex as those which send the motion, according to the principles previously stated.

"It ought, then, to be evident that the sensitivity of perception depends on the structure of the organ. Do not, therefore, be any longer astonished in seeing that not all individuals are equally impressed by the same phenomenon—nor, above all, that different animals on the evolutionary scale may see or not see what we, ourselves, can perceive in every detail. Inferior animals can only be impressed by the elementary motions derived from the least complex molecules, corresponding to the ones that form their bodies.

"The sensitivity of an animal, the intelligence or instinct, does not depend on the mass and the vital principle, but on the fineness, the variety and the multiplicity of the molecules that constitute its organs. The more numerous and varied they are, the greater aptitude they will have to collect the motions arriving from every direction, and the clearer and more numerous the impressions themselves will be.

"Why do all bodies appear to us with their own colors? Simply because their molecules are diverse and the motions of those molecules are different. The more motions there are, the more sensations there are. Why is one individual not impressed in the same fashion as another by the same color? Because the molecules of its organs are not aggregated identically to those of its neighbor— and the same for sound, for touch, for all the impressions that there are.

"Animals, we may be sure, do not see as we do, do not judge size or color as we do. Even within the human species, there are no two people whose impressions are identical. No two people ever see precisely at the same moment, hear at precisely the same instant. The difference in time gives an idea of the difference in the constitution of their senses.

"Thus it never happens that two astronomers, however experienced they are, observe the passage of a heavenly body at the same moment; one sees it a little sooner or later than the other. The error can be as much as a second. For each individual, a different time is required for the transmission of molecular motion to be effected. Your soul instructs your arm to raise itself; it takes a fraction of a second for the mechanism to obey; for your neighbor, it will be a different fraction of a second. In a word, the speed of transmission varies incessantly from person to person.

"Have you noticed that it is sufficient to look at someone for their eyes, after a few seconds, to meet yours? The effect is instinctive. It is the soul of the person you are looking at that obeys yours, always through the intermediary of a material agent, in this case light.

"You project upon a person's eye the motion[57] that reaches you from the Sun; that motion stimulates the retina, and then the brain of that person. This motion is different from the one that the other receives directly from the Sun; your retina has modified it in passing. The person therefore senses a distinct impression, wishes to know the source, and looks in the direction from which the particular motion comes.

"If the person's constitution is such that she[58] can enter into harmonic vibration with you, she will look at you more and more. The two of you will bring yourselves closer and closer to unison, and then great sympathy, your nerves vibrating synchronously. The molecules of the two bodies become animated with identical motions and the organs, which are only an assemblage

---

[57] Parville: "We know that light is merely the motion of the outermost atoms of bodies transmitted by the intermediary of independent atoms in space." For a long time, following various classical sources, it was thought that sight was a matter of active transmission as well as reception; Ziegler and Parville evidently still share this perspective.

[58] In Parville's text the use of the pronoun *elle* at this point merely reflects the fact that the noun *personne* is feminine rather than specifying the sex of the person concerned—a crucial linguistic difference between French and English that often causes some slight difficulty to translators. As Parville obviously has a female other in mind in this instance, however—he is, in effect, providing a quasi-scientific explanation for "love at first sight"—it is entirely appropriate to use "she" rather than substituting the neutral but grammatically dubious "they." I have adopted the same policy in the following argument regarding what would now be called hypnotism, because 19th century "magnetism" was usually a matter of male magnetizers influencing female subjects.

thereof, live the same life. The popular expression *their two hearts beat as one* will be entirely verified; it is thus that love can be born from a glance.

"If, on the contrary, the molecular constitution is such that the motions can never coincide and enter into unison, it is discomfort that the gaze will produce: natural antipathy.

"The connection produced by the luminous movement can be extended and considerably augmented by the molecular motions of other organs of relation; a hand placed on a hand is sufficient to further hasten the harmonic vibrations of bodies, and, in consequence, the similitude of impressions and thoughts.

"People are astonished by magnetic phenomena; they cannot imagine how one person can influence another from a distance. People have preferred to consider magnetism as a kind of trickery, scientists laughing at it; it is, however, gentlemen, a definite branch of an exact science.

"When two people are in unison—which is to say that their equally-stimulated nerve-threads are vibrating in unison—as external motions govern sensations, it is sufficient for the stronger to think of something for the weaker to have the same thought by repercussion; it is a veritable telegraphy.

"Nevertheless, as external objects also transmit the motions of their molecules, if the person who is receiving is not isolated from these foreign impressions, she will confuse the sensations emanating from these different sources, exactly like a telegraph receiving a large number of dispatches at the same time. Even so, she will conserve a vague and indecisive notion.

"Magnetizers get around this difficulty. When the connection is made and the subject's thoughts are already somewhat obedient to yours, you order her to sleep. You isolate her thus from foreign influences, and your thoughts become hers. Your two souls communicate, and your soul, instructing hers, makes her body move as if it belonged to you.[59]

"I said just now that you order her to *sleep*. What is the sleep that you can produce in this way? Gentlemen, it has been repeated endlessly that sleep is the image of death. Psychologists have opposed that expression vigorously; the idea is false. Nevertheless, the soul is never more independent than during sleep, and, in consequence, never finds itself closer to the state it will recover in death. It is enclosed in the body, but no longer in command of it, no longer making use of it. Sleep is, therefore, the time during which the soul is no longer in communication via the body, save in an accessory manner, with the external world.

"The body has to repair, on a daily basis, the loss of vital force that it expends in its external labor; the vital principle diminishes; the soul can no longer make the machine obey. It is a sailor whose ship is adrift, for lack of a rudder.

"The body rests, the soul remains awake but is no longer linked with its surroundings; it no longer sees; it meditates on its memories; it combines; it anticipates; no

---

[59] Parville's belief in "somnambulism"—what would nowadays be called hypnotism—was apparently based on experience. An article of his translated for the *Pall Mall Gazette* in the 1890s recalls an occasion during his American expedition when he allegedly put a number of Native Americans into a somnambulistic state, in which they imitated his actions and gestures slavishly.

longer tormented by external impressions, it acquires an incomparable power and activity of judgment.

"During this time, all the vital force is employed in reconstructing the body, repairing the day's wear and tear. In certain individuals, somnambulists, the soul conserves enough authority over the body to make it function, but usually without putting it into direct connection with the external world.

"What does the magnetizer do now, gentlemen? When the organization of his subject permits, he commands her to sleep, exactly as he would if the body of the somnambulist were his own. The soul obeys; the subject sleeps, and the magnetizer has only to telegraph his will.

"The less massive a body is, the more rapidly the magnetic effects will be produced, since there is less mass to control. It is for this reason that weak and small people are more impressionable than others. There will always be more rapidity and finesse in the conception of a nervous organization than any other, precisely because of the predominance of the vital force over the matter.

"Materialists, who confuse the vital principle with the soul, have certainly not considered these facts, which falsify their opinion. They are astonished by the fact that, although we do not have an exact notion of the Divinity, our ideas revolve eternally in the same circle. How? Can our sensations arrive from anywhere else than matter, that which we can see or touch? Our soul only sees and is only capable of judging according to the notions acquired by our organs. Our sensations never get away from that; we cannot, therefore, go any further by the method of positivism. If the soul did not exist, we would not have that very faculty of expressing ideas other than those given to us by sensations directly produced by the material world.

"Besides, the idea of God and the soul emerges incessantly, and gathers force as our external impressions weaken, ending up dominating all our thoughts. This is necessarily the case, in fact, because, the more vital energy is lost, the more the soul withdraws into itself, belonging more to itself and less to the body.

"I could offer more arguments, but Mr. Newbold is becoming impatient, seeing time moving on, and I only wanted to say a few more words in order to make it clear that everything I have said applies to the vital principle and not to the soul, which is eternally independent of matter.

"Finally, gentlemen, remember that, although motion and matter make and transform organisms, matter and motion require a creator. The hand of God, gentlemen, is manifest throughout the universe."

(Applause.)

Mr. Newbold: "Mr. Haughton has the floor."

Mr. Haughton: "Just a word to Mr. Ziegler. I do not insist on anything with regard to the entirely novel conclusions he has just expressed, but only that, since matter can organize itself—according to him—he prove it experimentally."

Mr. Newbold: "Mr. Haughton, we shall once again be drawn...."

Mr. Ziegler. "No, Mr. President, a minute's grace, not to convince Mr. Haughton but so as not to leave his objection without a response. I say that, by putting appropriate matter in the presence of appropriate mater, I can still produce organisms today. If I do it and demonstrate it, my honorable colleague will affirm that the organisms came from pre-existing germs. He will remind me of Monsieur Pasteur's experiments in France.

"In my turn, I shall say that the facts ascertained by Monsieur Pasteur prove absolutely nothing, and I would be able to demonstrate that if time were not lacking. I will add that Mr. Haughton, like Monsieur Pasteur, attributes the production of inferior organisms to impalpable germs. One does not see them, one merely presumes them, he says; I do exactly the same myself. There is no longer a germ; there are organic molecules so tiny that they evade the eye; these molecules, in aggregation, form the organism.

"Here the point of departure is the vital germ, the issue of the animal; there it is the similarly invisible corpuscle formed directly by organic matter in decomposition. All Monsieur Pasteur's experiments support my interpretation just as well as his, and I have several other experiments which, while remaining favorable to my views, contradict his theory. Mr. Haughton and I, however, could argue about these infinitesimal entities for a long time; I prefer to pass on today, to an experiment that will permit me to tighten my argument further. This time, Mr. Newbold will not reproach me for my developments."

(Laughter and other noises.)

Mr. Newbold: "The inhabitant of Mars, gentlemen!"

Mr. Rink: "I would like to point out to the assembly that the preceding discussions also show that because creatures are dependent, in terms of their structure and superiority, on the state of matter on each planet, they follow its evolution. In that aspect, they are not irrelevant to the question before us."

Mr. Greenwight: "Mr. President, we are very close to a conclusion; all that remains, in fact, is to establish how the aerolith was able to reach the Earth from a neighboring planet. Mr. Owerght is scheduled to speak, and I claim the floor on his behalf, in the name of astronomy. Tomorrow, though—tomorrow!"

Mr. Owerght: "I thank my honorable vice-president, and I shall put myself at the assembly's disposal tomorrow."

LETTER XIII

Mr. Owerght's speech. What an aerolith is. The part and the whole: bolide and asteroid. Collisions between heaven and earth. An unexpected cannonball. Vassal and suzerain. Can the Moon hurl stones at the people of Earth? Absolute negation of astronomers. Can a more powerful planet bombard the Earth? How we are imprisoned on each world. Nothing outside. External forces. How everything can be explained. The bolide is a mountain. How the Earth robs Mars.

Mr. Newbold: "Mr. Owerght has the floor. I must remind you, gentlemen, that I am obliged to close our discussions tomorrow; I cannot therefore recommend too insistently that you must each be brief."

Mr. Owerght: "Mr. President, I will only need a few moments. My illustrious colleague, Mr. Greenwight, has established perfectly that only one planet, in the extremely remote epoch of the aerolith's fall, was physically able to retain a creature conformed like the one we have before our eyes.

"The mummy cannot be terrestrial in origin; it comes from space, and all the data of physical astronomy agree in identifying the planet Mars as its source. My present role is very simple; it is a matter of checking that result and seeing whether it is mathematically possible.

"Now, I shall not hide the fact that, at first glance, it seems impossible—and all the astronomers will share my opinion.

"What, in fact, gentleman, is an aerolith? Is it to a *part* or a *whole* that we give the name *bolide*? What is a bolide? That question is no easier to answer. I shall not list all the hypotheses made by scientists here; I shall give the most generally-accepted opinion.

"A bolide is a planet in miniature. If you return to the considerations developed, you will see immediately that they are extremely primitive planets, of a relatively great age, long incapable of any evolution of living beings. Life has doubtless arisen there, but so briefly that only the most primitive organisms were able to appear.

"These bolides, or planetesimals, move through space in obedience to the same laws as large planets. Created at the same time, governed by the same forces, they describe their closed trajectories around the central world, the Sun.[60]

Now, let us suppose that the path the bolides follows around the Sun might cut across the one that the Earth follows, and let us suppose, too, that our planet might be passing through the junction point at the moment when a bolide is heading towards it from its own direction. In industrial parlance, they are two railway trains threatening to engage the same track, which they are approaching at a slant. There will inevitably be a collision. The bolide, which is a mere fly by comparison with the terrestrial mass, will crash into the ground without the Earth's inhabitants experiencing the least shock.

"If the Earth passes before or after the bolide, but at a relatively small distance, it can still have an effect on

---

[60] Although only a handful of asteroids were discovered in the first half of the 19th century new ones were reported every year from 1847 onwards, so it was widely accepted by 1864 that there might well be thousands or millions of them, many of which must be too small for telescopic detection, and that these were the most probable source of meteorites.

it, attracting it in exactly the same way that a piece of wood placed on the surface of the water in a draining bath is drawn towards the plug-hole. The Earth attracts the bolide, which is deflected from its path and, instead of turning around the Sun, begins, like an obedient vassal, to go around the Earth until it is precipitated on to its surface.

"Finally, it might be the case that even though the bolide passes too far from our planet for the latter to take possession of it, the Earth will influence it; it might even draw it into the atmosphere, but it will end up escaping.

"We should consider these bolides as similar to planets and not as enormous projectiles launched, as some would like to believe, by lunar volcanoes, because the velocity with which the move excludes any question of lunar origin. The Moon would never have enough power; its volcanoes could never constitute artillery sufficiently powerful to hurl such cannonballs at such a speed. A projectile launched from the Moon would arrive on Earth with a velocity of 11 kilometers per second. Now, the smallest bolides progress with a speed of about 30 kilometers per second.

"When a bolide grazes the Earth it penetrates into its atmosphere, and the resulting friction warms its surface enough to make it red hot. That high temperature modifies its structure; unequal expansion causes it to break up, or, at the very least, obliges the mass to hurl forth fragments which fall to the ground. These are aeroliths.

"The meteoric mass discovered by Messrs. Paxton and Davis presents all the physical appearances of an aerolith. However, none so voluminous has ever been found before. Its existence in the midst of ancient strata, although very remarkable, has absolutely nothing extraordinary about it, and is not at all discordant with what we know. This block, detached by the Earth at the moment of a bolide's passage, has been covered up by recent deposits. What makes it extraordinary, however, is this mummy, whose form is so bizarre, and these relatively well-fabricated vases, which have been found within its mass.

"Either the bolide had inhabitants, and everything can thus be explained, or it did not, and the block must have been torn away from an inhabited planet—which is much more difficult to imagine.

"Now, it has been proved that a bolide of this sort could not be inhabited. Life cannot arise, or, at least, perpetuate itself on such infinitesimal worlds. Furthermore, it has also been demonstrated that the planet Mars is the only one that could have possessed similar inhabitants. Thus, it is necessary to come back to this proposition: the mummy and the aerolith have come from the planet Mars. How? It is here that the difficulty of finding an answer becomes considerable.

"That a bolide circling the Sun might fall to Earth is a fact and is explicable, but that a block of stone belonging to another planet might escape that planet to travel to another would be absolutely inadmissible, as everyone will quickly see.

"Is not a planet merely the result of all the forces that draw atoms in space towards a given center? There are as may planets as there are targets to aim at and attain. In addition, everything that exists around planets tends to be concentrated there from the moment of their origin. This property of matter is very familiar; on Earth, we call it gravitation; in consequence, far from having any tendency to escape, any body placed on a planet tends to remain there, and to remain there without any effective ability to leave.

"But, you might object, why could not some volcanic force succeed in throwing a block of stone far enough from a planet for it to enter the field of action of another world? Why could a Martian volcano not have hurled this enormous projectile high enough for it to be attracted by the Earth?

"Evidently, those who have put this hypothesis forward, with respect to the Moon or Mars, have not taken the way in which worlds are generated into consideration.

"What kind of force can launch an aerolith into space? Could it not come from the reactions of internal matter that is still incandescent? Now is not this force the transformation, with a certain diminution, of the primitive force that condensed the atoms in space? How could that diminished force be capable now of pushing the atoms further away than whence they came? The equivalence of the mechanical force in each case demonstrates the absurdity of the hypothesis.

"No, it is impossible that any sum of atoms placed on a planet could, under the action of that planet's own forces, travel to a neighboring planet. I posit that proposition as fundamental.

"So, gentlemen, we still have to ask ourselves how the inhabitant of Mars arrived on Earth.

"It is as well to observe that, in the preceding theorem, it is clearly specified that a planet cannot lift anything from its surface by means of *its own forces*. But I see absolutely nothing impossible in admitting that a planet might lose mass under the action of extraneous forces. Here, and here only, I believe I can see a solution to the puzzle of the marvelous transportation of the aerolith and its mummy.

"Let us suppose, in fact, gentlemen, that the aerolith we now possess constituted the summit of one of the highest mountains on Mars. Let us suppose that a bolide like those which intersect the Earth's field of action passed very close to Mars in a remoter epoch—close enough to brush the summit of a mountain.

"The bolide has to be a cannonball of enormous force, which breaks and carries way anything that gets in its way. It encounters the peak of a mountain, breaks it, and carries it away, pushing it in front of itself and communicating its own speed to it. Note that there is nothing mathematically impossible in this. The shock, with respect to the mass of the aerolith, is quite insignificant; this bolide was considerable. Perhaps slightly deviated from its route, the enormous globe would nevertheless have continued on its way into space.

"It would be a great mistake to consider it strange that the detached mountain-peak did not fall back after the impact. Not at all: throw a piece of paper into the path of a moving wagon, and the paper will remain stuck to it, and the same is true of increasingly heavy objects if the speed of the wagon or the projectiles is increasingly great. There is nothing extraordinary about it. The peak of the Martian mountain and the bolide will soon be no more than a single whole; the mountain peak would have been a veritable aerolith for the bolide's inhabitants, if it had any.

"It now remains to explain the block's fall to Earth.

"The bolide, deviated by Mars, doubtless eventually adopted a trajectory cutting across the orbit of Earth closely enough to be influenced by its mass. The Martian bolide would have become the Earth's bolide. The block would have leave the bolide's field of action to enter that of the Earth, and would have finished up falling to the surface like a contemporary aerolith.

"As for the inhabitant found inside the meteoric mass, it is evident that he did indeed belong to Mars. Buried on the summit of a mountain with his ornamental objects, this inhabitant of our neighbor was undoubtedly an important person. A great savant, perhaps, who asked to be interred far from the world, above his peers? Who can tell? Perhaps he was an astronomer, a geometer to whom his compatriots were indebted for the discovery of the laws that regulate the universe. The inhabitants of Mars certainly never imagined that we might one day have their Newton or Kepler on our world!

"Thus, gentlemen, for my part, it does not appear to be impossible that, by virtue of entirely fortuitous circumstances, a block of stone might be torn away from one planet by the passage of a bolide and thrown back on to another. From this specialist viewpoint, although I cannot prove absolutely that this was the case, I can no more deny absolutely that it could have occurred. In the presence of the curious proofs accumulated by my colleagues, that result is almost as a confirmation."

(Murmurs. Considerable applause. Individual conversations.)

The president's hand-bell has some difficulty in re-establishing silence.

During the last part of the session, the floor was taken, in turn, by Messrs. Wintow, Rink, Ziegler, G. Mitchell, etc. The discussion ranged from the ethnology of planetary races to comparative physiology and the bizarre form of the inhabitant of Mars. I am not sending you the details, which I had a great deal of trouble grasping, and which, moreover, will not be of any interest to your readers. Suffice it to say that the assembly finished by reaching agreement on the point that the triangular form of the mummy's head must have resulted from the pressure to which it had been subjected, compressed as it was in its calcareous envelope. As for the little trunk hanging from the forehead, it is evidently the nose; it communicates with the back of the mouth. The more precise drawings that I am finishing at this moment will give you a good idea of the details.

LETTER XIV

Don't trust newspapers. Uproar at Paxton House. Who presides by night in Mr. Newbold's stead? Salamec on trial. The infusoria of Mars. In which we resuscitate on Earth the animals of other worlds. Mr. Wintow must be dreaming. Sensation. Mr. G. Mitchell of Frankfurt. The key to the plate. Mr. Owerght's mountain is found. What the inhabitant of Mars is. A tour of inspection. American generosity. Good news. The inhabitant of Mars arrives in France. Conclusion.

The debates have been brought to a conclusion by of a new discovery and a striking confirmation of the theoretical views expressed in this arena. This has, of course, nothing to do with the absurd rumors that have probably reached you in advance of my letter, and which owe their source to a rather amusing adventure.

Five or six days ago, at a moment when all Paxton House was sound asleep, and Mr. Newbold was snoring as loudly as the east wind rattling the logs of the cabins—I was in the room next door—there was a sudden loud noise downstairs. Windows shattered, all the dogs started barking, and red flames illuminated the recently-constructed buildings.

Everyone immediately got out of bed, thinking that we were under attack.

I was one of the first ones down, and, to my great astonishment, I saw absolutely nothing out of the ordinary except for a great fire burning outside the door of the conference hall, which shed a sinister light upon the trees and the buildings.

"What's that?" I said to Mr. Paxton

The dogs were yapping increasingly loudly, and hurling themselves furiously at the entrance door of the conference hall.

"Here's a clue that will doubtless help us," he answered, as he went into the hall, kicking out right and left to clear away the dogs.

We followed him. Everything appeared to be in order, and the most complete silence reigned in the room. We were about to leave when we heard a hoarse cry behind us.

At the same time, Mr. Paxton drew his revolver from his belt and turned round.

We had not gone far enough the first time. Like him, we retraced our steps.

At the conference-table, in Mr. Newbold's chair, a small, hunched black creature was majestically seated, grimacing frightfully in the light of the torches. It was writhing madly, stretching out its arms, twisting its body and shaking its head with incredible vigor. This fantastic individual was evidently imitating president Newbold.

We were stupefied.

In front of the conference table, the mummy had disappeared. The coffin, placed almost vertically during the day, had fallen over, coming to rest upside-down.

What could possibly have happened? Had the mummy woken up? Did we have the resuscitated inhabitant of Mars before our eyes? What would the academies say? Fallen from Mars, resuscitated on Earth!

The individual continued gesticulating, no less furiously, and surveyed us disdainfully. The torches only startled it slightly, and it addressed its singular mimicry preferentially in our direction.

I can still see it in the semi-darkness, its eyes flashing fire. We were a long way from the mummy's dark cavities!

Our error could not last long. The pretended inhabitant of Mars, seeing us advance, suddenly jumped several meters, releasing another cry more strident than the first, and leapt unceremoniously on to the secretary's table, overturning Mr. Newbold's hand-bell, which began tinkling immodestly, in spite of the late hour.

Mr. Paxton put his revolver back in his belt and burst out laughing.

The inhabitant of Mars was a large monkey of which he was particularly fond, and which he had an awful habit of taking everywhere with him.

Salamec had seen Mr. Newbold and his colleagues agitating since the beginning of the debates through the windows of the hall, and he had been determined to have his turn presiding over the assembly.

He had broken a couple of windows, knocked over a few benches, set the plate from the aerolith rolling over the ground along with the fossilized tomb, and installed himself, in the midst of the hubbub, in the president's seat, doubtless demanding the profoundest silence.

As for the fire, it is probable that, by way of imitation, he wanted the festival to be complete, and had lit a big bonfire in the middle of the courtyard. That morning, in fact, the workmen had been burning patches of dry grass that were encumbering the borders of the habitation.

How had Salamec lit the grass? That was the one thing we were unable to determine, and which caused considerable anxiety to his owner. He is, in fact, fearful on that account that Salamec might take it into is head one day to set fire to Paxton House and all its outbuildings.

News of the adventure got around. As always, it has been amplified; the marvelous has been mingled with it, and an Indianapolis newspaper naively informed its readers that, in the very midst of the debate, the mummy had suddenly reawakened, to the great amazement of the assembly. All the gossips in the city were carried away by this unexpected news. They swore, in their turn, that it had stood in front of the president and demanded the floor. The majority of the commission's members had made for the door.

Someone will write to you some day to tell you that the mummy itself has just left on the last steam-packet, and that it will disembark at Saint-Nazaire. Here, as with you, the public has its weaknesses and weaknesses have their public.

No more joking. The last session has taken place today and, I repeat, has removed any doubts that anyone might still have had regarding the origin of the interplanetary habitant.

Messrs. Paxton and Davis have put a stop to the work; the aerolith is almost entirely pierced through and nothing interesting has been found therein. Mr. Wintow, however, called attention to a very curious fact.

"Gentlemen," he said, "Mr. Rink and I have extracted inferior organisms, clearly identifiable, from a few fragments from the aerolith. Better still, these little creatures, extremely tiny and preserved in the interstices of the rock, where the heat cannot have been extremely elevated, are very similar to our infusoria. Here they are, gentlemen; everyone may observe them at his leisure.

"I shall even repeat a striking experiment, which we carried out yesterday with complete success, and which will certainly interest Mr. Ziegler very greatly. I dampen these obviously inert and immobile organisms with a little warm water...you see that these, gentlemen, are gradually beginning to stir, move and return to life, just as the little infusoria, tardigrades and rotifers, which inhabit the gutters of our roofs, die and return to life when the Sun dries them out or the rain moistens them. Here, I am forced to think, with Mr. Ziegler, that it really is a certain quantity of motion that these creatures need to come back to life. The water has given them the requisite conditions, and the organism resumed its functioning."

"This provides further evidence that life in the planets really does have the same causes everywhere, and that the evolutions of matter are the same everywhere.

"In conclusion, gentlemen, do I need to observe that here, before your very eyes, are organisms that have been asleep for thousands of years, which have arrived here from another planet, which can still be resuscitated, visibly alive, as if we had been able to go to examine them in place and explore their primitive environment? Who would have dared suggest that we would ever possess creatures borrowed from a neighboring planet here on Earth?"

Mr. Stek: "We shall send them to our acclimatization society."[61]

---

[61] The transplantation of crops from one part of the world to another, and the consequent establishment of colonial plantations, was a highly significant component of global commercial enterprise in the 18th and 19th centuries; botanical gardens proliferated in support of such endeavors in both Europe and America, and "acclimatization societies" undertook intensive studies of the practicality of such transplantations in order to facilitate colonial enterprises.

Mr. Newbold: "I shall bring the discussion to a close, gentlemen, but first I shall give the floor to Mr. G. Mitchell, who has some extremely important details to communicate to us."

(Loud murmurs. Individual conversations.)

The hand-bell is shaken; silence is re-established.

Mr. G. Mitchell, distinguished anatomist from Frankfurt; a fine orator, in spite of a falsetto voice: "Gentlemen, I certainly would not wish to detain you here any longer if I had not been fortunate enough, with the aid of my excellent friend and colleague Mr. Sieman, to discover irrefutable proof of the ultra-planetary origin of the mummy, and if I were not therefore able to crown the edifice that you have built so sagely and skillfully.

"Gentlemen, the aerolith really has fallen from Mars, and we have before our eyes a veritable man of that planet. Not one of you will leave this place, I hope, without being utterly convinced. Of what the clear and remarkable theories of my illustrious colleagues have permitted us to prejudge, gentlemen, I can give you material and indelible proof."

(Sensation! Movement! Profound silence.)

"Already, several among us have carefully examined the silver plate that covered the tomb. It seemed that we ought to be able to discover the secret of this envoy of other worlds thereupon. That was no mistake, gentlemen.

"Yesterday, Mr. Sieman and I decided to study the bizarre lines engraved in the metallic surface. First of all, the worlds depicted with their relative distances—the Sun, Mercury, etc.—are the focus of attention; then, higher up, the palm-like trees and the rhinoceros, permit no thought of anything but a world, and a world that is not our own.

170

"One of the first arguments that weighs in favor of Mars, as you know, is the large volume of that planet in the design on the plate. It is suggestive of local pride. Who, however involuntarily, does not regard his homeland with a complaisant eye? And for any inferior intelligence, is not size or extent a characteristic of superiority?

"This reasoning is certainly not worthless, but it is only hypothetical. I have two remarks to make which will, I think, confirm it sufficiently to settle the question.

"Below and further to the left of the planetary globes, which you can doubtless distinguish here, examine carefully these two groups. Here are four round black marks, and here, facing them, two more.

"Now, in the middle of the space between these two groups, notice a very clear circle at least ten times as large, in whose interior is inscribed a series of lines curved in a fairly regular manner.

"The first group represents, without any doubt, the Sun, then Mercury, Venus and the Earth, all planets describing their trajectories around the Sun on this side of Mars. The second group represents Jupiter and Saturn, planets rotating around the Sun beyond Mars. Finally, in the center and quite apart, the planet Mars itself. Why, on this occasion, this double designation? Why, in addition, categorize those which, on Earth, we call the inferior planets and the superior planets?

"It is indisputable that the grouping of the two series can only have been made by an inhabitant of Mars. If the intelligent being which designed these figures had lived on Venus, for example, it would have categorized the stars thus: the Sun and Mercury, then the Earth, Mars, Jupiter and Saturn. I do not think anyone can refuse to see the light emerging from this simple distribution of planets, according to their distances from Mars itself.

"An astronomer on Mars would have ascribed the center of the system of the universe to the planet that he inhabited, just as the original terrestrial astronomers ascribed it to the Earth. In addition, this justifies the excessive volume of the depiction of Mars.

"Finally, the characters traced in the center of the large circle, representing the planet Mars, undoubtedly designate it as the pivot of the system.

"There is even more, gentlemen—I said that doubt was not possible! See for yourself. Mr. Sieman has distinguished all around the central disk, which separates the two groups, a large circle, effaced for the most part, then a second, the a third, much clearer, and finally a fourth, half-covered by bizarre lines whose significance escapes us. Is it not necessary to see these circles as the orbits of planets? It is quite certain that the astronomer of Mars believed that the Sun and all the other worlds rotated around him.

"I have said that I was in the process of demonstrating the astonishing precision of the theory's deductions. Listen to this; it is better than everything that has gone before. Mr. Owerght claims that the mummy has been torn away from the summit of a mountain by a bolide deviated from its course. Mr. Owerght is correct.

"By washing the plate with nitric acid, Mr. Sieman caused to appear, to our great astonishment, very faint lines that can be followed with a microscope. They are very extensive and occupy the greater pat of the plate. We have made a reproduction on a large scale, which we now set before your eyes.

"It is impossible, in following this line, not to recognize the vague contours of a veritable mountain. Two

172

fairly clear peaks still surmount it to the right, and give it a great height. The line is lost as it curves to the left, where it is also hidden by a palm-tree. Is not that, gentlemen, the massive mountain anticipated by scientific reasoning?

"There is better still; follow the escarpments of this tortuous line, then descend abruptly, following the vertical; who will not admire the astonishing concordance of facts which conclusions already reached?

"At the base of the plate, near the middle, are engraved—this time profoundly—four strokes forming a rectangle; fix your attention upon them.

"Mr. Oupeau was the first to have the honor of studying the lines that intersect in this document of sorts. After washing it twice with acidic water, he showed us quite distinctly a very faint image of the plate itself—the plate that we now have in our hands.

"There is more and better to come, gentlemen. Near the base, a little lower down, one can quite easily make out a form that must be that of the mummy laid out in its coffin. Even lower down—this time outside the rectangle—a sequence of closely-packed strokes can be distinguished, incomprehensible to us, but which are certainly letters and must form words.

"Finally, lower still, but half-effaced, one can, with a little imagination, make out several mummies analogous to the specimen that has fallen to Earth, which seem to be contemplating the summit of the mountain.

"In case anyone thinks that I am letting myself be carried away by imagination, ever one of you, gentleman, will be able to verify it.

"I can only see these designs as a faithful representation of the mountain. At the base, a plaque must doubtless have been embedded in the rock, representing the coffin and the image of the dead man; these characters are simply an inscription, whose meaning unfortunately escapes us completely, but which would doubtless have been placed there to remind future generations of a name henceforth immortal.

"Perhaps we now have at Paxton House a great king whose power would have astonished the peoples of Mars. Perhaps, and we are inclined to believe it, we possess one of the initiators of astronomy on that world, of which we know so little. From the summit of the mountain that you see here, the great scientist might have discovered what were then believed to be the veritable laws of the universe.

"In any case, it is indubitable that the mummy had a spectacular renown and an immense influence in his own country; perhaps he was even venerated as the equivalent of a demigod, as he might have been supposed to be by the creatures who are bowing before his remains. One can probably measure the importance of the person by the importance of his sepulcher.

"He must have been buried far away from the other mortals of Mars, at the summit of the mountain, in such a way that he looked down on his peers after his death from as great a height as he had looked down on them in life.

"Gentlemen, who can tell whom we might have here, before us, and what glory of another epoch and another world we have been contemplating since Mr. Paxton's discovery?

"Who knows whether, at this very moment, while we are all gathered in this arena, out there, the scientists of Mars might not be discussing on their own behalf the strange disappearance of this great illustration of ancient times? For the base of the mountain must still be there, along with its commemorative plaque, and—unless a tradition has revealed the event of which the country was a theater—they must be lost in conjectures regarding the problematic existence of a sepulcher of which no trace remains. The archaeologists of Mars must have spent more than one sleepless night over these incomplete vestiges of another age, these singular remains of the planet's first humans.

"Is it not strange that it has perhaps been given to the inhabitants of the Earth to discover, before those of Mars, the key to the enigma—or, at any rate, to possess irrefutable proof of a historical fact that will forever escape them?

"The scientists of Mars still have the base of the mountain; but what we have is a faithful representation of the entire mountain, the sepulcher and the dead man. We know, better than they do, what happened on their world, and we now possess an extremely well-preserved specimen of their first humans! There is much truth in the dictum that one is not always a prophet in one's own land.

"Gentlemen, it was given to our century and to the New World to become the cradle of the greatest scientific discovery of times past and present. I bow to destiny, and I thank God for choosing us—his humble creatures of the terrestrial world—to learn that we are not isolated in space, and that every world that shines in the sky is a new oasis of life and of eternal creation."

(Loud applause. People crowd around Mr. G. Mitchell.)

Mr. Newbold, agitating his hand-bell: "Gentlemen, has anyone anything to add to the interesting communication that you have just heard?"

(Silence.)

"In that case, I will briefly summarize the debate and pass on to the assembly's vote.

"The conclusion of the geological considerations developed by my illustrious colleagues is that the aerolith discovered by Messrs. Paxton and Davis cannot have a terrestrial origin.

"The conclusion of the arguments invoked by Mr. Greenwight is that a creature of the nature of the one that has been brought to the Earth can only have come from one planet, Mars.

"Mr. Ziegler, by his fine analysis of the conditions of existence on each world, and Mr. Owerght, by his argument regarding the transportation of matter through space, have permitted us to consider it as not impossible that creature from one world might fall upon another.

"Finally, the interpretation, so unexpected and so remarkable, that Mr. G. Mitchell has just drawn from his examination of the plate with Messrs. Sieman and Oupeau, provides a complete confirmation of the theoretical views expressed in this arena.

"Such are the consequences to which we are led by the logic of the facts.

"It remains for me to submit this conclusion to the assembly: Yes, the creature discovered by Mr. Paxton definitely comes from the planet Mars."

The urn was passed and the conclusion was adopted; there was one blank paper.

Mr. Newbold: "You have heard the assembly's decision, gentlemen; our work is therefore terminated. The doubts have been dispelled and we can only anticipate the confirmation of our research by the entire scientific world. The verbal proceedings of our sessions will be distributed to the academies of the New and Old Worlds.

"It remains for me, on my own behalf, to thanks my illustrious colleagues for the constant attention that they have been willing to lend us, and for their assiduous cooperation, which have made my task so easy. I shall carry away from here a memory that will never be effaced.

"The Paxtons have asked me to express their wholehearted gratitude and to ask each one of you to accept, before we part, this commemorative medal. It bears on one side a faithful reproduction of the inhabitant of Mars, and on the other, the date of our meeting. Each of them will remain for posterity a sort of irrefutable testimony of the Commission's debates and judgment.

"Finally, gentlemen, the sanction of the august body of European scientists is worth a great deal to us. It is necessary that petty party rivalries and paltry preoccupations of pride and nationality should give way to respect for the truth and the love of science. Thus, the Paxtons have resolved to sacrifice their discovery and send the remains of the inhabitant of Mars to Europe. It is necessary that doubts should not spring forth anywhere, and that the most enlightened centers of the Old World have material proof that will permit them to check our assertions.

"America will keep the aerolith, the amphorae and the metal rods. Europe will have the mummy and the plate.

"It is with pride, we admit, that we can inscribe on the Commission's dispatch this testimony of our liberality and our devotion to science:

"FROM THE NEW WORLD TO THE OLD WORLD."

(Loud applause; Mr. Paxton is congratulated.)

Mr. Newbold: "Gentlemen, the Institut de France and the Royal Society of London seem to us to be worthy in every respect, by virtue of the high esteem they enjoy and their incontestable authority, of becoming the depositories of the remains so miraculously discovered on American soil. To England, therefore, the plate and its convincing designs! To France, the cradle of art, literature and good taste, the inhabitant of Mars!"

(Thunderous applause. Prolonged cheering.)

"This unanimous support, gentlemen and dear colleagues, will be the most welcome recompense to the Paxtons for their generosity; for us, there will be a new and glorious page to add to our scientific annals.

"We have done our duty, and we can await the judgment of posterity with confidence."

Postscript. Almost all the members of the Commission are leaving tomorrow morning. Travel arrangements are being made. I shall follow shortly thereafter.

A very pleasant surprise was reserved for me, about which I want to tell you before closing this letter. I am the one who will have the honor of going to Europe to offer the interplanetary man to your Académie des Sciences. I already have the authority in hand, along with Meswrs. Newbold and Paxton's instructions.

I shall soon be able to thank you personally for the publicity that you have been wiling to give our debates. I shall reserve the first fruits of our discovery for you; you shall be the first to see the inhabitant of Mars.

I hope to arrive, with my precious baggage, by the end of December at the latest. Until then.

Paxton House, September 27.

POSTFACE

We waited—and with what impatience!

December passed—nothing. Then January, February and March.

Our disappointment was complete when, on waking up a little while ago, our eyes finally fell upon a letter, open as usual.

What a letter! What a stupefying signature!

Richmond, March 15

Are we forgotten, then? For two full months you have had the inhabitant of Mars in your hands, and not a word from you.

Mr. Newbold has asked me to tell you how grateful we shall be if you will translate, in your turn, the debates to which the interplanetary man will have given birth in the bosom of the Institut de France.

Assuredly the most devoted of your colleagues,

Henri de Parville.

My signature—my own signature!—no doubt about it!

This letter....

Have I, then, written it myself? The ink is still fresh.

What about my American correspondent, though?

What? He has sent me the inhabitant of Mars? But reader, I swear that I have received nothing from him; I declare that I have never seen it with my own eyes.

Then...?

I must have been my own correspondent for six months; all the letters must be from me to myself. Unknown to myself, I must have written to myself by night what I read by day....

Come on, that's impossible!

I'm dreaming.

And what about the drawings deposited in my desk?

Let's see, reader, enlightened reader...is it really the case that no one has found a man in an aerolith anywhere on Earth?

Can it be the case that Mr. Greenwight the astronomer does not exist? Can it be that Mr. Newbold the geologist...that Mr. Rink...that Mr. Ziegler...???

Felix qui potuit rerum cognoscere causas.[62]

April 1, 1865.

---

[62] "Happy is he who knows the causes of things." The line is from Virgil's *Georgics*.

Afterword

Parville, Hetzel and the Origins of French Scientific Romance

The idea to expand Parville's hoax articles into a book might conceivably been the publisher's rather than the author's; Hetzel was always an entrepreneurial publisher, who routinely approached authors with proposals rather than waiting for them to come to him. Whether that was the case or not, though, it is interesting that *Un habitant de la planète Mars* was issued by Hetzel, at a time when the publisher was actively promoting a variety of what would now be called "science fiction."

Hetzel's first major project as an editor, *Le Nouveau Magasin des Enfants* [The New Magazine for Children], which he had stated for Hachette in 1843, had become remarkable by virtue of his powers of persuasion, which drew such influential writers as George Sand, Charles Nodier, Alexandre Dumas, Alfred de Musset and Alphonse Karr into a field into which they might not otherwise have strayed. Hetzel had been exiled to Brussels in 1851 after Louis-Napoléon's *coup d'état*—like many other fervently Republican literary men he had accepted a government post after the 1848 revolution—and had not returned to Paris until 1859, but he had remained active in the interim, publishing several important works by his fellow exile Victor Hugo. In the early 1860s, however, he was setting out anew to rebuild his career, more determined than he had been before to make a real impact in French publishing, despite the ever-vigilant eyes of the Emperor's censors.

Although Hetzel had retained a strong interest in the publication of children's fiction—and in writing for that audience, as P.-J. Stahl—he was in the process of spreading his wings, and his experimentation with fiction celebrating the joys of technological progress was part of that expansion. In

1863 he had persuaded Alexandre Dumas' struggling protégé, Jules Verne, to develop a series of newspaper articles that he had written about ballooning—alongside the unsuccessful poetry and drama that he then considered to be his true vocation—into an adventure story. Hetzel subsequently signed Verne up to write works on a regular basis for serialization his new periodical, *Magasin d'Education et de Récréation* [The Magazine of Education and Recreation]—which, unlike his Hachette venture, was intended to provide entertainment for the entire family rather than simply providing material for parents to read to their children—and subsequent publication in volume form. Although much of the fiction Verne subsequently produced for Hetzel was straightforward action-adventure fiction featuring expeditions into remote regions of the globe that were then being explored for the first time, Hetzel encouraged him to make the most of the technological means that were facilitating real exploratory ventures and providing a substantial part of their motivation.

Verne followed up *Cinq semaines en ballon* (tr. as *Five Weeks in a Balloon*) with the even more adventurous *Voyage au centre de la Terre* (1864; tr. as *Journey to the Center of the Earth*). Hetzel sent a copy of *Voyage au centre de la Terre* to George Sand, who was inspired by it to write *Laura ou le voyage dans le cristal* (1865; tr. as *Journey within the Crystal*) and Verne also followed it up in 1865 with *De la Terre à la Lune* (tr. as *From the Earth to the Moon*). In the same period, Camille Flammarion, who had recently published a speculative account of *La pluralité des mondes habitées* [The Plurality of Inhabited Worlds] (1862) and a fascinating comparative survey of *Les mondes imaginaires et les mondes réels* [Real and Imaginary Worlds] (1864) began to use semi-fictional frameworks in his own exercises in popularization, in the works subsequently collected in *Récits de l'infini* (1865-69; book 1872; tr. as *Stories of Infinity*). Parville's work thus took a significant place within the flurry of activity that lent French scientific romance its first significant impetus, creating a thriving genre whose products were routinely responsive to one another where there had previously been little more than a smattering of disconnected works.

The credit due to Hetzel as a founder of the Vernian tradition ultimately came to seem slightly tarnished, partly because his publication of many of Verne's works in a "family magazine" resulted in his being widely regarded as a writer of juvenile fiction, and partly because he was known to have Verne's rejected futuristic fantasy *Paris au XXème siècle* (written 1863; published 1994; tr. as *Paris in the 20th Century*). It seemed, therefore, that he had initially encouraged Verne's imagination only to subject it to an unreasonably tight rein thereafter. *Voyage au centre de la Terre* remained Verne's most imaginatively ambitious work, and after writing *Vingt mille lieues sous les mers* (1870; tr. as *Twenty Thousand Leagues Under the Sea*) and *Autour la Lune* (1870; tr. as *Around the Moon*), he mostly settled into the writing of more conventional adventure stories, with only occasional excursions into science fiction.

When Verne's futuristic fantasia was finally published in 1994, however, it turned out that Hetzel had been quite right to reject it, in spite of the striking quality of some of its technological anticipations, because it was so relentlessly downbeat and peevishly hostile to technological progress. No matter how carefully confined Hetzel's notion of scientific romance was, he was certainly an enthusiastic advocate of exploration and progress, and he judged—correctly—that what was, in essence, a blatantly self-pitying reaction to Verne's earlier literary failures would not assist his future career in the slightest. Parville's stratagem for dealing with the possibility of life on Mars, on the other hand, fitted in reasonably well with Hetzel's restrained prospectus, and Hetzel might well have entertained considerable hopes for it, until he actually saw the complete manuscript. Parville, alas—like many scientists—turned out to be profoundly uncomfortable with the narrative techniques of fiction, and simply could not do what Verne was able to do so brilliantly in transmuting the substance of popular journalism into the substance of popular fiction.

Even with the residual publicity of the successful hoax to assist it, Parville's profoundly awkward book had no chance of scoring as big a hit with the contemporary audience as Verne's adventure stories—but that does not make it uninteresting, especially to modern readers; in addition to the originality of its central idea, which establishes it at the very head of a long tradition of fabular discourses on life on Mars, it provides a remarkable panoramic snapshot of a particular world-view that seemed perfectly viable in mid-19th century France, and was tacitly to underlie and shape the distinctive development of French scientific romance. It was probably not an influential book in itself—indeed, it probably had less influence on subsequent writers of French scientific romance than Parville's non-fictional writings, some of which appear to have been used as source-materials by Albert Robida—but the ideas it summarizes certainly retained their influence. It was, therefore, a significant foundation-stone of the nascent genre, and fully deserves to be recognized as such.

Parville, the Popularization of Science and the Plurality of Worlds

In the late 1870s, the relevant volume of the first edition of Larousse did not hesitate to say that Parville was already the most highly-esteemed *vulgarisateur* [popularizer] of science of his generation, but he was not the most popular then or thereafter; that accolade always belonged to his eternal rival, Camille Flammarion. Flammarion's reputation and esteem within the scientific community were, however, somewhat undermined by his insistent Spiritualist faith, which routinely intruded into his heroic efforts to popularize the fruits of the science of astronomy. Parville permitted a similar intrusion, briefly and somewhat unexpectedly, in *Un habitant de la planète Mars*, but he construed "spiritualist" in its philosophical sense—as the antithesis of "materialist"—rather than with reference to the newly-fashionable religion imported from America, for which Flammarion served as an advocate and propagandist. Parville was careful not to allow any confusion to arise thereafter between his modest version of spiritualism, as summarized by Mr. Ziegler, and Flammarion's, in which communication with disembodied souls via mediums was a matter of routine. In spite of his somewhat archaic faith in "magnetic somnambulism", therefore, Parville thus preserved his reputation as a scientist much more securely.

Oddly enough, even though Flammarion was much more given to producing cosmic visions than Parville, he never managed to produce anything quite as succinctly thorough as Parville's brief foray into fiction. The longest of the *Récits de l'infini*, *Lumen*, which was expanded for publication as an independent book in 1887, uses a dialogue form that is just as awkward as Parville's, and eventually covers more narrative ground, but it is considerably more long-winded and the greater part of its bulk in devoted to a narrower range of problems. The heart of Flammarion's cosmic vision, and his primary narrative concern, was the notion of cosmic palingenesis—the possibility that immortal souls might be serially reincarnated on different worlds—but Parville was careful to stop short of any such assertion, or even the serious consideration of any such possibility, and it was therefore unnecessary for him to attempt any narrative description of the cosmic odysseys of questing souls. Parville did, however, share Flammarion's considerable fascination with the debate about the plurality of worlds, which had always held a particular significance in French intellectual history, and the separation of their views took place against a substantial common background.

Parville's interests and ideas also had some significant points in common, and equally significant contrasts, with those of the leading English popularizer of science in the mid-19th century, Robert Hunt. Hunt had made an earlier start, and he died some time before Parville, but he was heavily involved in the founding and development of England's first dedicated mining school and he played the same role with respect to the English Great Exhibitions as Parville played with respect to the French *Expositions Universelles*. Hunt, too, dabbled in fiction in the early part of his career, producing the novel *Panthea: The Spirit of Nature* (1849); like Parville, however, he decided that he was unsuited to such work and gave it up in order to concentrate on more earnest endeavors.

Panthea employs a more orthodox narrative form than *Un habitant de la planète Mars* or *Lumen*, but its core is a cosmic vision, albeit one that relies far more on geology and biology than astronomy. Like Flammarion, Hunt had been influenced by Humphry Davy, who had also included a cosmic vision in a collection of philosophical dialogues, *Consolations in Travel* (1830), but Hunt refrained from the kind of extraterrestrial flight of fancy featured in Davy's work, preferring to concentrate on the composition of the Earth and its biology. When he wrote *Panthea* Hunt was—like Davy—a confirmed Creationist, although he subsequently read *The Origin of Species* and became a fervent admirer of Charles Darwin. To an even greater extent than Camille Flammarion, however, Parville continued for some while after 1859 to think of evolution in strictly Lamarckian terms; there is no trace of the notion of natural selection in *Un habitant de la planète Mars*, in spite of its sympathy for Pouchet's ideas and Mr. Ziegler's insistent contradiction of Pasteur's supposed disproof of them.

Hunt was not alone in refusing to follow up the extraterrestrial aspects of Davy's vision; the genre of British scientific romance that got under way in 1871 remained mostly Earthbound for 20 years, obsessed with future wars and extrapolations of anti-Darwinian anxiety. The fact that Parville, in spite of having no interest in cosmic palingenesis, was nevertheless drawn to consider extraterrestrial possibilities was undoubtedly due to the fall of the Orgueil meteorite, but the fact that the Orgueil meteorite had such an imaginative impact in France, as well as a literal one, is itself symptomatic of the fact that the question of the plurality of worlds seemed much more important in France than it did in England. It is worth noting that even Edgar Allan Poe's *Eureka*, which is primarily concerned with the imaginative impact of astronomical discoveries, has very little to say about the possible population of other worlds—and American scientific romance similarly remained Earthbound until the 1890s.

What Parville's cosmic vision does share with Poe's is its entrancement by analogies between the macrocosm and the microcosm and images of harmonic eternal recurrence. It is possible that Parville had read Charles Baudelaire's French translation of *Eureka*, which was published in 1864, before writing *Un inhabitant de la planète Mars,* and, if so, might have taken some inspiration from it—but whether he did or not, the most significant precursor of Parville's book was undoubtedly a much earlier work, already established as a classic of French scientific literature and still regularly reprinted in the 19th century: Bernard de Fontenelle's *Entretiens sur la pluralité des mondes* (1686; tr. as *Conversations on the Plurality of Worlds*).

The debate about the plurality of worlds had begun as an abstruse theological dispute. The early church fathers tacitly accepted the Ptolemaic model of "the world" endorsed by Aristotle, which placed the Earth at the core of a sequence of concentric spheres containing the Sun, the Moon, the planets and—at the outer circumference—the "fixed stars". This was widely accepted as the whole of Creation, but some theologians—most notably Origen (c185-254) in his pioneering attempt to compile an encyclopedic account of theology, *De Principiis*—felt that it was an insult to God's omnipotence to asset that he had only created one world, and that he might, if not must, have created many more. Because Origen was opposed in this matter by the ultimately more prestigious St. Augustine, the idea of the plurality of worlds was set aside and largely forgotten for more than a thousand years, but it was revived in 1440 by Nicholas of Cusa in *De Docta Ignorantia*, which proposed that the universe ought to be as infinite as God Himself, and therefore ought to contain an infinite number of worlds of equal status, of which the Ptolemaic world-system would merely be one.

The renewal of the argument was initially regarded as an arcane item of scholastic controversy of no practical import, essentially akin to such notorious hypothetical questions as that of how many angels might be accommodated on the head of a pin (another question to which Parville makes oblique reference, with his tongue in his cheek). Its nature and significance were transformed, however, when Copernicus popularized the heliocentric model of the solar system, which relegated the Earth from the center of Creation to the status of one of several planetary bodies, all of which might qualify as "worlds" in their own right. Nicholas of Cusa had not been accused of heresy, but the followers of Copernicus were soon declared unorthodox, and when astronomical evidence began to mount up that Copernicus was right, the debate became ferocious.

Giordano Bruno, who suggested in 1584 on the basis of "the principle of plenitude" that God must not only have populated all of the worlds in our solar system but all the worlds in all the other solar systems in the infinite universe—because their creation would otherwise have been pointlessly wasteful—was burned at the stake, although his reputation as a martyr to science was soon eclipsed by Galileo, who had actual telescopic discoveries to oppose to the Church's technologically-unaugmented faith. John Kepler and Christian Huygens added further astronomical observations favoring the new version of the plurality of worlds; significantly, both of them attempted to use fictional frameworks to dramatize their idea and make them more readily understandable, thus launching a parallel literary tradition. Kepler's posthumously-published *Somnium* [Dream] (1634) and Huygens' *Kosmotheoros* (1698; tr. into both French and English as *Cosmotheoros*) provided the foundation-stones of a genre of cosmic visions, to which Humphry Davy, Robert Hunt, Edgar Allan Poe, Camille Flammarion and Henri de Parville—not to mention Félix-Archimede Pouchet—were eventually to make their significant contributions.

The plurality of worlds debate was further popularized in the French language by Pierre Borel in *Discours nouveau prouvant la pluralité des mondes* [A New Discourse Proving the Plurality of Worlds] (1657), but it was Fontenelle's much more elegant *Entretiens* that put the issue firmly on the national cultural agenda. The "conversations" are actually a series of educational lecturers delivered by a savant to a curious young lady, and the arguments they set out are as clever as they are succinct; their conscientiously light-hearted and witty surface provided a polite mask for their highly controversial subject matter, which was still likely to attract condemnation from a Romanist Church sufficiently powerful in France to place its proponents in danger.

Fontenelle's best-seller was followed shortly thereafter by the fragmentary publication of an expurgated version of Savinien Cyrano de Bergerac's *L'autre monde* (1662; tr. under various titles, most definitively as *The Other World*, although the individual parts are far better known as *A Voyage to the Moon* and *The States and Empires of the Sun*), a far more flamboyant work of fiction championing the same ideas and subjecting opponents thereof to scathingly sarcastic criticism. Unfortunately, the work remained fragmentary, most of its second part and all of the third being lost, although the parts that were published were eventually reissued in unexpurgated versions. Both Fontenelle and Cyrano drew extensively on *Le monde* [The World] (1632), a relatively informal work by René Descartes, which presented a more thoroughgoing opposition to the Church's Aristotelianism than Copernicanism provided in isolation—but Descartes had abandoned the popularization of science after writing it and retreated from publishing in French to orthodox scholarly publication in Latin of more abstract philosophical notions.

Descartes' speculative account of the origin of the solar system in *Le monde* was greatly elaborated by Pierre-Simon de Laplace in *Exposition du système du monde* [Exposition of the System of the World] (1798), which became the standard work to which Flammarion, Parville and other 19th century visionaries referred back. Descartes was not the only great philosopher to devote attention to the production of cosmic models—Immanuel Kant's *Allegemeine Naturgeschichte und Theorie des Himmels* (1755; tr. as *Universal Natural History and Theory of the Heavens*) had already surpassed his work before Laplace took up the thread, and was more successful in its visionary anticipations—but Descartes had the greater literary influence, especially in his own country. Such planetary tours as Marie-Anne de Roumier's *Voyages de Milord Céton dans les sept planets* [Voyages of Lord Seaton in the Seven Planets] (1765) took what scientific basis and justification they had from him and his followers.

In the debate's original theological context, it was taken for granted that, since God had made man in His own image and humankind was a key element in Creation, any other worlds that He had created must also be inhabited by human beings. The post-Copernican writers who began to vary this thesis initially did so very modestly, and primarily in one single respect: that of size. Nicholas Hill's *Philosophica Epicurea, Democritiana, Theophrastica* [Epicurean, Democritian and Theophrastican Philosophy] (1606) argued that the size of created individuals must vary in proportion to the size of their worlds, and most later writers agreed. Giordano Bruno had already suggested that there might be some variety, without going into detail, as did Pierre Gassendi in his posthumously-published *Syntagma Philosophicum* [Collected Philosophical Writings] (1658). Cyrano de Bergerac took the idea further, albeit in a blatantly satirical spirit, but restricted himself to what was to become another common ploy: the notion that intelligent beings might be formed like Earthly animals, like those that had long featured in fables

The German writer Otto von Guericke, writing in 1672, seems to have been the first to suggest that God's infinite creative imagination might have disposed Him make to the population of other worlds infinitely variable as well as infinitely numerous. In France, the assumption that the intelligent inhabitants of other planets were likely to be human persisted throughout the 18th century, although Voltaire's *Micromégas* (1752) was one of numerous works that made telling use of presumed differences in size, adding in differences in sensory perception for good measure. Parville not only clung hard to the notion that humans would arise almost everywhere, but attempted to build a new scientific explanation in support of the notion that the most significant variation between the human species of different worlds would be a mere matter of size.

Parville's theory of convergent evolution does leave room for the evolution of human species far beyond the stage currently represented on Earth, even though he refrains in his novel from offering any substantial suggestions as to what improvements future human species might embody. Although his original hoax article flirted with the introduction of some minor physical differences—most notably the trunk-like nose—he deliberately de-emphasized them in the expanded text. It was, in consequence, left to Flammarion, in the later dialogues in *Lumen* (first published in 1868-9) to grasp the full implications of the notion of evolutionary adaptation to physical circumstances and to begin—in spectacular fashion—the invention and depiction of authentically alien intelligences.

In respect of the population of a plurality of worlds, Parville's stereotypy was at the tail end of an old tradition, while Flammarion was at the head of a new one, but modern readers might judge that the retrospective credit balance is redressed by Parville's careful avoidance of the embellishment of cosmic palingenesis. The notion that immortal souls might not be bound to their own worlds, being free to roam the vast post-Copernican plurality of worlds as their various hosts died, experiencing further incarnations on other worlds, had first been put forward by Huygens in *Kosmotheoros*, but was re-popularized in France by Charles Bonnet in *Contemplation de la nature* [The Contemplation of Nature] (1764). It was quickly borrowed by Louis-Sébastien Mercier, a devotee of Jean-Jacques Rousseau and the great pioneer of futuristic utopianism, who used it in his visionary short story "Nouvelles de la Lune" (1768; tr. in a Black Coat Press edition as "News from the Moon") before Bonnet expanded and elaborated the thesis in *Palingénésie philosophique* [Philosophical Palingenesis] (1769). The idea was also taken up by two other enthusiastic followers of Rousseau: Nicholas Restif de la Bretonne, in the epistolatory novel *Les posthumes* (written 1788; published 1802); and Jacques Bernardin de Saint-Pierre—the author of the best-selling sentimental novel *Paul et Virginie* (1788)—in the philosophical treatise *Harmonies de la Nature* [Harmonies of Nature] (1815).

It is conceivable, given Parville's own strong interest in the idea of harmony in nature, that what put him off the idea of cosmic palingenesis was not its inherent implausibility so much as the political leanings of its followers. As a man who fancied himself an aristocrat, in spite of his humble origins, Parville was zealously right-wing in his political affiliations—most of the periodicals he wrote for were conservative—and he was certainly not an admirer of Rousseau's radical disciples. This obviously did not prevent him from allowing the proudly Republican Hetzel to publish his work, but might nevertheless have tempered his eagerness to follow in the footsteps of writers who were so firmly associated with the left. (Humphry Davy, who had unashamedly introduced cosmic palingenesis into his own cosmic scheme, had been regarded in his earlier days as a key practitioner of what the disapproving English Tory press called "Jacobin science", because he had a tendency to hang out with such dangerous revolutionary types as Joseph Priestley, Samuel Taylor Coleridge and Robert Southey.) Whatever the reason, though, Parville turned out to have been wise in his avoidance of that particular imaginative recourse.

Geology and Palaeontology in the mid-19th century

It may be appropriate, in considering the historical context of Parville's hoax, to add a brief prefatory comment on the contemporary state of geological and paleontological science in 1865. His own educational background was in geology, albeit geology of a practically-orientated sort, and he was obviously very familiar with the controversies that had long been raging in that science.

Throughout the 18th century, the interpretation of record of the Earth's past contained in rock strata had been interpreted within a catastrophist framework, which attributed the apparent pattern of change to periodical upheavals such as the Biblical Deluge and volcanic eruptions. This framework had been broadly accepted by the leading French geologist and palaeontologist of that century, the Comte du Buffon, whose *Théorie de la terre* (1749; tr. as *The Theory of the Earth*) and *Époques de la nature* (1778; tr. as *Epochs of Nature*) remained standard works in France. Parville's references to ancient catastrophes in the text of *Un habitant de la planète Mars* and his use of terminology illustrate the extent to which Buffon's ideas still permeated French thought, and his off-hand references to Charles Lyell seem symptomatic of a certain hostility to the English school of geology whose members believed that they had rendered catastrophism obsolete.

The uniformitarian revolution in geological thought had been launched by the publication in 1795 of James Hutton's *Theory of the Earth*, which proposed that the Earth had been slowly reshaped over a vast reach of time by the forces of erosion, deposition and consolidation. The idea was inevitably controversial because it made utter nonsense of the Bible-based chronology which, according to Archbishop James Ussher, famously set the date of the Earth's creation in 4004 B.C. Although many previous geologists, including Buffon, had realized that the Earth must be far older than that, they had made their amendments piecemeal rather than wholesale, and relatively diplomatically; Buffon had been careful to keep the Biblical Deluge, even though he had reduced it to the status of one of a long series of transformative catastrophes extending over an unspecified time-span. The uniformitarian thesis represented a qualitative rather than a merely quantitative shift in perspective.

Hutton's thesis was greatly elaborated and brought to a crucial maturity by Charles Lyell in *Principles of Geology* (1830), but Lyell's work was regarded with a certain anxious suspicion in both Catholic France and Protestant America. Radical as their thinking was in other respects, Humphry Davy and Robert Hunt were both profoundly uneasy about the implications of uniformitarianism, and they both tried to affect a reconciliation of sorts between uniformitarian data and creationist faith, just as Parville does.

The problematic status of fossils had become increasingly acute in the context of this geological controversy. The multiplicity and variety of known specimens increased by several orders of magnitude during the 18th century, and fossils played a major role in convincing Buffon and others that the world must be far older than Biblical theorists claimed. From the 1750s onwards, discoveries of giant fossil mammals became increasingly commonplace, especially discoveries of mastodon bones in America. Such finds provided abundant data for George Cuvier's classic *Recherches sur les ossements fossiles* (1812; tr. as *Researches on Fossil Bones*), which set out the principles by which an entire skeleton might be hypothetically extrapolated from a relatively meager set of specimen bones—or, indeed, from a single bone. The manner in which Parville's fictitious scientists attempt to extrapolate their relatively meager discoveries is in the Cuvier tradition, although they do not have occasion to use his actual method of reasoning.

In the 1820s, the principal focus of paleontological attention shifted to much older, but equally gigantic, fossil reptiles excavated on Britain's south coast, which prompted fiercely heated debates in London between Creationist naturalists and uniformitarian geologists. The term "dinosaur" was coined in 1841 by Richard Owen to assist in the classification of these new discoveries, although it had been partially anticipated in France by Etienne Geoffroy Saint-Hilaire's *Recherches sur des grands sauriens* [Researches on Giant Saurians] (1831). The focus of attention switched again in the 1860s, however, when abundant specimens began to turn up in the American West, soon initiating a strong popular interest in fossil-collecting and fervent competition between rival "dinosaur hunters." Although the fiercest and most notorious of the resultant feuds, between Edwin Drinker Cope and Othniel Charles Marsh, did not break out until 1873, the competition was already evident and newsworthy when Parville was inspired to concoct his hoax; it provided the backcloth against which "news" of a surprising fossil find in Colorado might seem plausible. The same popular interest in fossil reptiles had also played a major role in inspiring the underworld enclave featured in Jules Verne's *Voyage au centre de la Terre*.

In view of the significance of fossil finds to the context of plausibility in which his hoax appeared, it might seem odd that the attendees at Parville's hypothetical conference have very little to say about the implications of actual fossils. Indeed, it is briefly noted at one point that their "old school" chairman, Mr. Newbold, is actively antipathetic to any mention of fossil humans of terrestrial origin; presumably, in spite of his name, he had conservative inclinations similar to Parville's, and would not have approved of Verne's decision to feature a giant humanoid alongside the much remoter relics conserved in Verne's imaginary underworld. Parville is content to provide a theoretical reason why the animals of Earth's remote past might have grown to lager sizes than those still extant, and avoids material that might have seemed contentious to his readers. It is possible that he was advised to proceed in this manner by Hetzel; indeed, Parville's third letter gives the strong impression that he originally intended to make his fictitious scientific conference much more flamboyantly contentious that it turned out to be, and his book might have been far more exciting if he had. For whatever reason, though, he settled in the end for setting out views closely akin to his own, providing no substantial opposition save for a few relatively trivial and conscientiously polite objections. It is difficult to imagine things going so smoothly in any actual conference of the period in which deeply entrenched opinions were under threat.

Postscript

Interestingly—especially in view of what Mr. Wintow reveals in the final chapter of Parville's book—it now appears that Parville's was not the only hoax inspired by the fall of the Orgueil meteorite. In 1962, Bart Nagy re-examined the ample of the chondrite that had been sent to Chicago and found what he took to be microfossils within it. Having rushed news of the discovery into print, however, he was contradicted by other scientists who examined the specimen; S. L. VanLanrigham, C. N. Sun and W. C. Tan published analyses in Nature in 1963 and 1967 demonstrating the terrestrial origin of the seeds that Nagy had mistaken for fossils—a demonstration that as all the more newsworthy because the identification of the seeds also established the likelihood that the contamination had not been accidental. Although it is far too late to be sure, it seems probable that someone deliberately tampered with the Chicago specimen before it left France, intending contemporary scientists to "discover" the "fossils".

This tale acquired another twist a few years later, by which time it had been established that there really were meteorite fragments on Earth that had been dislodged from Mars by asteroid impacts, much as Mr. Owerght had suggested in Parville's novel. In 2002, it was alleged that one of these "shergottite" meterorites, found in the Antarctic, gave the appearance of containing microfossils. Again subsequent examination by other scientists resulted in the claim being discounted as a hopeful illusion. By that time, alas, hardly anyone remembered Parville original hoax regarding a Martian meteorite, or his novel in which the meteorite turns out to contain miscroscopic animals capable of regeneration.

There is, of course, a world of difference between microfossils and a mummy, but it is worth noting that Martian mummies also have a shadowy 20th century history, not merely in acknowledged works of fiction, but also in association with the orgy of speculation that followed the publication of a NASA photograph of a "face" on the Martian surface. Although the appearance was an accident, resulting from shadows cast by a rock formation, it gave rise to a flurry of supplementary "telescopic discoveries" similar to those once provoked at Percival Lowell's Flagstaff observatory by the popularization of the notion that there were canals on Mars.

Although most 20th century images of Martian mummies relate to fictitious mummies discovered on Mars, one spectacular exception is to be found in an exhibition mounted in Brussels in 2000, of specimens from the "forbidden collection" of the explorer Alexandre Humboldt-Fonteyne, exhumed from a private museum and organized for display by Michel de Spieglière. The high-point of the exhibition was a group of mummified Martians that Humboldt-Fonteyne had recovered from the Anasazi ruins in New Mexico—which are, as they saying has it, not a million miles away from James Peak, Colorado. Michel de Spieglière is, in fact, a pseudonymous artist, and the entire "Humboldt-Fonteyne exhibition"—including its extraordinarily elaborate guide-book to the life and discoveries of the imaginary explorer—was a cleverly-compiled, magnificently-detailed and artistically-brilliant hoax.

Although Parville's article and book, along with their subsequent echoes, must still be judged to constitute contradictory evidence with respect to the common claim that truth is stranger than fiction, this subsequent history certainly emphasizes the fact that the relationship between the two is more intricate, and more ironic, than is sometimes appreciated.

BLACK COAT PRESS

J.-M. & R. Lofficier (eds.). *Tales of the Shadowmen 1: The Modern Babylon*
J.-M. & R. Lofficier (eds.). *Tales of the Shadowmen 2: Gentlemen of the Night*
J.-M. & R. Lofficier (eds.). *Tales of the Shadowmen 3: Danse Macabre*
J.-M. & R. Lofficier (eds.). *Tales of the Shadowmen 4: Lords of Terror*
Xavier Mauméjean. *The League of Heroes*
Frank J. Morlock. *Sherlock Holmes: The Grand Horizontals*
C. Nodier, Beraud & Toussaint Merle. *Frankenstein*
Charles Nodier. *Lord Ruthven the Vampire*
John William Polidori. *Lord Ruthven the Vampire*
P.-A. Ponson du Terrail. *The Vampire and the Devil's Son*
Eugène Scribe. *Lord Ruthven the Vampire*
Brian Stableford. *The New Faust at the Tragicomique*
Brian Stableford. *The Stones of Camelot*
Brian Stableford. *The Wayward Muse*
Brian Stableford (ed.). *News from the Moon*
Villiers de l'Isle-Adam. *The Scaffold*
Villiers de l'Isle-Adam. *The Vampire Soul*
Philippe Ward. *Artahe: The Legacy of Jules de Grandin*
David White: *Fantômas in America*

NON FICTION
Jean-Marc & Randy Lofficier. *Shadowmen: Heroes and Villains of French Pulp Fiction*
Jean-Marc & Randy Lofficier. *Shadowmen 2: Heroes and Villains of French Comics*